Also by Tess Hilmo

WITH A NAME LIKE LOVE

SKIES LIKE THESE

TESS HILMO

MARGARET FERGUSON BOOKS
Farrar Straus Giroux
New York

Farrar Straus Giroux Books for Young Readers
175 Fifth Avenue, New York 10010

Copyright © 2014 by Tess Hilmo
All rights reserved
Printed in the United States of America
by RR Donnelley & Sons Company,
Harrisonburg, Virginia
Designed by Roberta Pressel
First edition, 2014
10 9 8 7 6 5 4 3 2

mackids.com

Library of Congress Cataloging-in-Publication Data
Hilmo, Tess.
    Skies like these / Tess Hilmo. — First edition.
        pages cm
    Summary: While visiting her eccentric aunt who lives in Wyoming,
twelve-year-old Jade befriends a boy who believes he is a descendant of
Butch Cassidy.
    ISBN 978-0-374-36998-9 (hardback)
    ISBN 978-0-374-36999-6 (e-book)
    [1. Wyoming—Fiction. 2. Aunts—Fiction. 3. Eccentrics and
eccentricities—Fiction. 4. Friendship—Fiction.] I. Title.

PZ7.H566Sk 2014
[Fic]—dc23
                                                           2013033675

Farrar Straus Giroux Books for Young Readers may be purchased for business or promotional
use. For information on bulk purchases please contact Macmillan Corporate and Premium
Sales Department at (800) 221-7945 x5442 or by email at specialmarkets@macmillan.com.

For Meagan, Eli, and Claire,
who stand at the precipice

1

Jade gazed out the car window at knee-high yellow grass rolling and bending across the prairie like waves in the ocean, crashing into black, jagged mountains off in the distance.

"That big craggy one is Grand Teton," Aunt Elise said, both hands tight on the steering wheel of her old Lincoln Continental. Jade wondered how her aunt could see over the dashboard, she was so short. "I've climbed it seventeen times."

Jade looked sideways at her aunt. She studied her wild, choppy hair poking out every which way, then dropped her eyes down to the knit vest and awful brown corduroy pants that ended a full five inches above her sandals. Jade tried to imagine her aunt climbing Grand Teton. "Mom didn't tell me you were a hiker."

"What did your mother say about me?"

That was an interesting question. Aunt Elise had moved to Wyoming seven years ago. Before that, she lived a block over from them in Philly, but Jade was only five when Aunt Elise had moved and couldn't remember much beyond the fact that her father always called her aunt "an unusual bird" and her mother always shushed him.

"She said you run a doggy dude ranch."

Aunt Elise wiggled her shoulders. "Indeed I do. Diggity Dog Ranch, the best in all of Wellington."

"How many doggy dude ranches are there in Wellington?"

"Well"—Aunt Elise hesitated—"just the one."

"That's quite the distinction then." Jade had to agree with her dad. Aunt Elise seemed a bit odd, and the last place Jade wanted to spend part of her summer vacation, or any time really, was Wyoming. She loved Philadelphia, with its classic architecture and historical significance. She loved knowing every twist and bump of sidewalk within her neighborhood, and how Mrs. Wilkins didn't mind if you picked a few raspberries from her bushes or how you should shop at Mr. Yee's market because his candy bars were always a dime cheaper than anywhere else.

"I can't believe you're finally here." Aunt Elise was smiling so wide her cheeks were about to split open.

"I can't believe it either," Jade said, slumping down in her seat.

"I was pinching myself all morning. I kept saying, Elise, you've been away from that precious niece for entirely too long. Today is the day you'll see her again."

Jade turned her head away from her aunt, toward the prairie grasses and flowers that spread out to the horizon. She had never seen so much open space. There was an occasional abandoned field or city park in Philadelphia, but they were still organized and gridded into allotted plots of land. Wyoming was seamless and vast.

"I see you're a fellow adventurer." Aunt Elise flicked a hand toward the tattered copy of *Robinson Crusoe* sticking out the side pocket of Jade's backpack.

"Mom gave it to me. She said it was one of her favorites."

"How far along have you gotten?"

"A little over halfway." Jade fiddled with the blue tassel of the bookmark.

"What do you think of it?"

"Robinson Crusoe doesn't seem very bright."

"What makes you say that?"

"Well," Jade began, pondering the story, "as I see it, he would have saved himself a mess of trouble if he'd listened to his dad and stayed in England."

Aunt Elise stared straight down the road. Jade couldn't tell what her aunt might be thinking, so she turned her head back to the side window and counted fence posts along the highway. They were strung together with rusty barbed wire, holding in auburn horses, grazing cattle, and the occasional sheep. She counted all the way up to twenty-one posts before Aunt Elise broke the silence.

"So you start reading the greatest adventure tale ever written but think it would have been better if he had stayed home?"

"Pretty much, but I'm not finished," Jade said. "It's just that this Crusoe guy never really considered how dangerous life might be for him as a sailor. He should have been more judicious."

"Judicious? What grade are you going into?"

"Seventh."

"Well"—Aunt Elise seemed to be measuring her words—"promise me you'll keep reading it, okay? You might be surprised how *judicious* Mr. Crusoe really is after you see all he does to handle himself on that island. It's impressive stuff."

Jade shrugged and went back to counting fence posts.

"Uh-oh, storm on the horizon." Aunt Elise was squinting at the sky.

Jade sat up and leaned forward. It was bright blue overhead, but dark clouds shifted and stirred off in the distance. "Those clouds are miles away."

"Weather moves fast across open land. That looks like a powerful front." A gust of wind swept across the prairie, flattening tall grasses in its wake and hurtling into the side of their car. "Hang on." Aunt Elise tightened her grip and sat up as tall as she could, as if that would make a difference.

Jade locked her car door and tugged on her seat belt. "It's only a little rain, right?"

The corner of Aunt Elise's mouth curled into a half smile. "Nothing about Wyoming is little."

Suddenly a crack of thunder split the sky. Darkness fell and dense rain poured from above. Lightning ripped across the western horizon.

"One Mississippi, two Mississippi, three Mississippi." Aunt Elise counted up to ten Mississippis before another explosion of thunder enveloped them. "That bolt landed two miles away."

"How do you know?" Jade asked, her voice trembling.

"Five seconds equals one mile. Start counting from the flash of lightning and stop with the thunder. That's the speed of sound."

The towering mountains Jade had been admiring were not visible anymore. Steel-gray mist shrouded the car and silvery raindrops—the fattest she had ever seen—battered the windshield with earsplitting thumps.

"Don't worry," Aunt Elise called out. "We'll make it."

How her aunt could even see the road through the storm, Jade hadn't a clue, but she seemed to know how to manage it. She swerved past rivers of rain and plunged through puddles that sent fans of water spraying out from the wheels. She watched the lightning and counted seconds before the thunder clapped above. "It has to get closer before it passes," Aunt Elise said. "One Mississippi, two . . ."

Crack.

"Excellent," Aunt Elise said.

Lunatic, Jade thought, squeezing her eyes shut. She should have been signing up for the summer reading program down at the library like she did every year. She should have been organizing the pantry and trying out new cookie recipes and playing mini golf with her friends. Anything other than being in the middle of nowhere with a woman she hardly knew. What were her parents thinking, sending her off like this?

"And there it goes," Aunt Elise said.

Jade tentatively opened her eyes and saw shards of sun slicing through the mist. The pelting rain slowed and slipped off the back of the car, like they were driving out of a car wash. She turned around and saw the storm moving on behind them.

"That was a good one," Aunt Elise said. "But it's over now."

Jade worried that wasn't true.

She was worried it had just begun.

2

Aunt Elise continued to drive past spacious fields, where black cows raised their chins up to the sky and horses ran wild, tails flicking behind them. Gradually, buildings began to speckle the land, growing closer together. Aunt Elise pulled off the highway and entered the sprawled-out town of Wellington. After weaving through a few blocks, they came upon a large gate; a wooden dog carved out of a massive tree trunk stood next to it like a sentinel. In its mouth hung a sign that read: DIGGITY DOG RANCH. Aunt Elise pushed a button on her car visor that opened the gate and Jade could see an adobe house with a flat roof and large front porch at the top of the driveway. "Home sweet home," Aunt Elise said.

The moment the gate closed behind them and the car started up the drive, a band of barking dogs appeared from around the side of the house, yapping and nipping at all four tires.

"How many are there?" Jade asked.

"Nine this week. Some'll go, some'll stay. There's no need to be afraid, they won't hurt you."

Jade tried to relax the muscles across her brow and force a smile. "I'm not afraid."

Aunt Elise turned off the car. "I'll get out first and provide a diversion. You can skedaddle into the house."

Jade unhooked her seat belt and pulled the silver door-lock knob up. That simple movement and its subsequent *click* brought all nine dogs running over to her side. They were shoving and nudging and vying for position. One massive brown dog stood as tall as the window and looked directly at Jade. His gray-pink tongue dangled out the side of his mouth. A smaller, curly-haired dog jumped up against the window, smearing muddy paw marks as he went.

Jade took a deep breath and started to open her door. The car was from sometime around the Paleozoic era and the doors took a little effort to get going. The moment it was ajar, black noses began pressing into the opening.

"Heel up!" Aunt Elise said, stepping around from her side of the car. The band of dogs scampered over and sat in a cluster at her feet.

All except the huge one. It stayed put, waiting for Jade.

"That's Astro." Aunt Elise was talking about the massive dog at Jade's door. "He's a bullmastiff. He's slow as January honey. Sweet like that, too. Reach your hand out for him to sniff and he'll step away."

"But his nose is so close to his teeth."

"He just wants to check you out."

Jade opened the door wider and reached a hand toward the dog. He ran his nose along her fingertips. It was cold and damp and the whiskers on his upper lip tickled her skin, sending a tiny jolt of delight shooting up her arm. The joy of it surprised her.

"I think you've made a new friend."

Jade forced the smile that had managed to creep across her face down into a serious expression. "Hardly," she said, feigning disinterest.

Aunt Elise shook her head. "When a dog like Astro decides to love you, there's no hardly about it."

Astro sat down with a snort as Jade eased out of the car. Coming across the prairie she had seen horses that weren't much bigger than this dog at her feet. "Is he one that will go?" Jade asked.

"Probably not. His owners brought him for a two-week stay three years ago."

"And left him?"

Aunt Elise pulled the luggage from the trunk and

wheeled it up to the front door. The dogs crowded and skittered around her feet.

Except Astro, who stayed right where he was, his attention fixed on Jade. She reached out, slid her hand across the dog's head, and scratched behind his left ear. He closed his eyes and heaved a deep sigh. Like her touch was the sweetest thing he had ever experienced. Like he had been waiting for it his entire life.

"I knew you two would get along. He's as glad you came as I am. You're going to like it here."

"Really?" Jade was always curious about people like Aunt Elise who seemed to know exactly where they came from and where they were headed and how they were going to dodge every obstacle the universe might throw their way. "How do you know?"

"Give me these few weeks, Jade Landers." Aunt Elise was grinning again. "I'll show you the Wyoming I love."

3

Jade should have let her expectations go when she first saw her aunt at the airport. She should have known there wouldn't be bearskin rugs and antlers hanging on the walls of Aunt Elise's house. She should have guessed she wouldn't be saddling up broncos or sliding turquoise rings onto all of her fingers.

"Kitchen's in back," Aunt Elise said, disappearing down a narrow hallway. "I put some stew in the Crock-Pot this morning. You must be starving after that long flight."

Jade stepped past her luggage and followed her aunt. The hallway was dark even though the sun was still shining bright outside, but she could make out a few pictures on the wall. One was of Aunt Elise at the summit of a mountain, possibly Grand Teton. Another showed two girls in plaid dresses and patent-leather shoes standing on some steps. Jade leaned in and looked at those girls. She guessed the younger one to be her mother. Aunt Elise was the oldest by seven years, which would make her fifty-one.

"Come eat and then we'll check in with your folks," Aunt Elise called from the kitchen.

Jade started to go, but noticed a gilded frame at the end of the hallway. It was her baby picture. The one where she was swaddled in a white crocheted blanket.

"You were an angel." Aunt Elise leaned against the kitchen doorjamb.

"Were you there?"

Aunt Elise came over to where Jade was standing. "Absolutely." She reached up and ran a finger along the frame. "I was there for all of your firsts—your first word, your first step, your first day of kindergarten."

Jade tried to remember her very first day at Martha Washington Elementary. She had a tattered, wispy recollection of her aunt standing at her mother's side.

Aunt Elise clicked her tongue twice. "I would like to introduce you to someone." A silver bullet of fur streaked past Jade's legs and up into her aunt's arms. "This is Copernicus. The dogs rule the outside. Copernicus rules the inside."

"Copernicus," Jade said. "I remember that name from my science class. Wasn't he an astronomer?"

"Yes, and do you remember what the original Copernicus is most famous for?"

Jade thought. "I think he was the one who first claimed the sun as the center of our universe."

"Correct!" Aunt Elise jabbed a finger in the air. "Everyone thought Earth was at the center of our planetary system. Copernicus challenged that assumption, and do you know what they did?"

Jade didn't have a clue.

"They judged him harshly because they didn't understand him. They were afraid of his different views and called him crazy." She shook her head. "Isn't that like people? To think we're the center of the universe? Come, let's eat."

Aunt Elise handed the cat to Jade.

"Oh," Jade said, fumbling with the bundle of fur. "I don't really do cats."

Aunt Elise disappeared back into the kitchen. Copernicus pressed his head under Jade's chin, purring like a locomotive.

"Chow's ready," Aunt Elise called out.

Jade pulled Copernicus away from her chest and set him down on the orange shag carpet. He eased between her feet, pressing his side against her ankles in a smooth figure-eight pattern. She stepped over him, careful not to trip, and into the kitchen.

Which was a sight to behold.

Paper stars bathed in silver glitter dangled from every inch of ceiling. Crammed in between the stars were Styrofoam balls painted in bright yellows, blues, and oranges.

"It's the solar system," Jade said, not able to take her eyes off the ceiling.

"It is. Roy made this for me. He snuck in one day while I was out and pinned all these up with fishing line. Pluto is represented as a full planet when it's really been demoted to a dwarf planet, and Saturn is off position, but it's pretty close. Can you imagine my surprise when I came home?"

"Who's Roy?"

Aunt Elise sat down at the kitchen table and began eating her bowl of stew. "That," she said, "I'll let you discover for yourself."

Jade joined her aunt at the table, still mesmerized by the art hanging over her head. A small fan buzzed on the counter in the corner, offering enough breeze to send the paper stars twisting and turning. And, as they did, the glitter sent tiny shards of color and light shooting out across the room.

It was spectacular.

"Eat up," Aunt Elise said between bites. "I'm no Food Network star, but it's hot and filling."

Jade's stomach rumbled. "I love watching the Food Network." She scooped a spoonful of potatoes and meat into her mouth. The moment her lips closed around the spoon, she knew there was a problem. It tasted awful, and bits of slimy, chewy fat replaced what she had thought was meat.

Aunt Elise looked up from her bowl and smiled.

Jade smiled back. "Mmmm," she said, forcing herself to swallow and ignore the gag reflex in her throat.

"I made enough to feed us for days."

"That," Jade said slowly, "is great."

Aunt Elise made a motion with her spoon, encouraging Jade to take a second bite.

Which she did. "I'm not very hungry," Jade said, forcing down the spoonful.

"Nonsense. You're like a chicken bone with a head. I'll fatten you up in no time."

The dogs out front began barking as the doorbell chimed.

"Excuse me." Aunt Elise left the kitchen for the front door.

Jade yanked her bowl off the table and placed it on the floor where Copernicus was stretched out, lazily thumping his tail against the sun-drenched linoleum. He lifted his head, sniffed the stew, and turned away. "So you agree," Jade said to the cat. She ran to the trash can in the corner and scooped the stew into an empty Cheerios box, being certain to close the lid and place a few crumpled napkins and wrappers on top. Then she put the bowl back on the table.

"Jade Landers, as I live and breathe. Coming to join us in the paradise of Wyoming."

Jade looked up to see a boy with a round, freckled face standing at the back door. He was in full cowboy gear—a wide-brimmed hat, pointy-toed cowboy boots, worn-out Wranglers, and an oversize silver belt buckle. "Do I know you?"

"Roy Parker. It's short for LeRoy, after the famous LeRoy Parker." He yanked off his hat and turned sideways, offering up a profile.

"And that is . . . ?"

A flash of shock passed across his eyes. "LeRoy Parker?" He was clearly distressed. "Better known as Butch Cassidy? Surely you people in Philadelphia have heard of Butch Cassidy!"

"How old are you?"

"Twelve, just like Elise told me you are."

Jade thought he looked short for twelve. "She's at the front door."

"I know. I rang the bell because I wanted to meet you on my own."

Understanding lit Jade's mind. "Oh, *Roy*. You must be

the one who made all of this." She waved her hands up toward the dazzling ceiling art.

A smile pulled across Roy's face. "Like it?"

"It's not bad."

Roy tilted his head at the Crock-Pot full of stew. "You didn't eat that, did you?"

"Pure poison."

"Hungry?"

"Famished."

Roy tugged his hat back on. Then he pulled a Butterfinger candy bar from his back pocket, stripped off the wrapper, and snapped it in half. "If there's one thing I've learned from my great-great-uncle Butch Cassidy, it's that a real cowboy should always help a damsel in distress." He lined up the halves of candy bar side by side and handed Jade the larger of the two. "Welcome to Wyoming," he said, warm as the day. "You've come just in time."

Jade shoved the Butterfinger into her mouth.

"That's strange," Aunt Elise said, coming back into the kitchen. Then she saw Roy. "Have you been up to your tricks again?"

"Roy was saying I came just in time," Jade said.

"Just in time for what?" Aunt Elise asked.

"That's what I was wondering."

Roy glared at Jade and then turned a smile on Aunt Elise. "Oh," he said, "you know."

Both Aunt Elise and Jade looked blankly at Roy.

"Just in time," he continued, stuttering and stumbling over his words, "to see the Wilsons' heifer calve. She's about to pop any day now."

"Gee. Glad I won't miss that," Jade said, sarcasm dripping.

Roy gave her the stink eye and mouthed something that looked like *later*.

"Well, you be sure to come tell us when their cow goes into labor," Aunt Elise said. "A person should see something like that at least once in her life. Wouldn't you agree, Jade?"

"At least once."

Aunt Elise stirred the stew in the Crock-Pot. "You want some chow, Roy?"

"Nah." He was tucking his already-tucked shirt into his jeans—clearly trying to show off his belt buckle. "I've got official business to attend to."

"Will we see you for stars tonight?"

"I wouldn't miss it!"

"What are stars?" Jade asked.

"You don't know what stars are?" Roy laughed. "You're more city than I thought."

Aunt Elise put a lid on the stew. "I think she was talking about the event more than the objects." She turned to Jade. "I have an observation deck on my roof."

"Nine-thirty?" Roy asked.

"Sharp," Aunt Elise said. "Bring your parents. We'll make it a party." She gestured up to the paper stars and Styrofoam planets that filled her ceiling and said to Jade, "If you think this is beautiful, you'll love the real thing. A night sky is the best Wyoming has to offer. Remember when you asked how I knew you'd love it here? Come up on my roof and see the stars, then you'll understand."

4

Jade had only climbed a few ladder rungs but she felt worlds closer to those early-evening stars just starting to poke through the slate-gray sky.

"I've never been on anyone's roof before," she said, stepping off the ladder.

"Most folks haven't, I suppose." Aunt Elise jostled two plastic beach loungers into the center of the flat roof. Jade noticed a small retaining wall along the perimeter. "But what fun is a vacation without some adventure?"

Jade eased onto one of the loungers.

"After I bought the house, I had this observation deck built," Aunt Elise continued, stretching out next to Jade. "From the street it may look like any other pueblo-style home, but come around back where the ladder is and you'll see it has a little more to offer."

The two settled in and stared silently at the sky as a silvery dusk fell into navy darkness.

When the last trace of daylight was gone, Jade took in the view above. "Wow."

"A tad different from below, right?" Aunt Elise scooted over and, under the softness of the sky, whispered, "Do you see the bright one off to the left? Now look slightly up and to the right. Can you see the one with the coppery-red glow?"

"Yes."

"That's Mars." Aunt Elise leaned in and pressed her warm cheek against Jade's. "So I can see your vantage point," she said. She took Jade's hand, folded her fingers into a point and reached it outward. "And this star over here marks the corner of the Big Dipper."

"My mom taught me about the Big and Little Dippers."

"That's a good start," Aunt Elise said, guiding Jade's finger to a specific star within the constellation. "Do you see how the handle of the ladle on the Big Dipper arcs over?" She was moving Jade's finger across the sky. "Follow that arc away from the Big Dipper to the brightest star you see. That is called Arcturus. You can remember it by saying, *The Big Dipper arcs to Arcturus.* It is one of the brightest stars north of the equator this time of year."

Jade was breathless. They had night skies in Philly,

even pretty ones, but nothing like this. The stars in Philadelphia towered high above the buildings and seemed impossible to reach. These were right at her fingertips. "I think I could grab that ladle if my arm was a little bit longer."

Aunt Elise let out a quiet laugh. "And that's how you get hooked. I came out to Wyoming to visit a friend seven years ago. One night, we found ourselves up on the roof of William's hardware store, looking at the stars."

"William?"

"Roy's dad. That was the night we met. A few of us had gone to see a play and when it was all over, he led us back to his store and invited us up onto the roof." She got all quiet, lost in memory. "I knew I wanted to spend the rest of my life under this sky, so I finagled my way out of the law firm I was tied to and started new."

"Never looked back?"

Aunt Elise paused. "No," she said. "I looked back plenty. There was good in both places."

Jade couldn't get over the view. "It's gorgeous."

"If you spend your whole life with your feet firmly rooted to the ground, you miss out on these moments. I'm telling you, Jade, skies like these make you believe you can do anything."

Just then, the dogs on the far side of the yard started barking.

"Parkers are here," Aunt Elise said.

"Yodel-ee-yo," a woman called out, coming over the top of the ladder and onto the roof.

Jade sat up and saw a tall, thin woman with yards of filmy fabric draped about her shoulders. Jade could see her clearly because she held a lantern in one hand, illuminating her sharp nose and chin and showing the purple and green of her wide, breezy shawl. Behind her, a short man with a round face and rectangular glasses stepped onto the roof. Then Roy came up behind his parents.

The moment they were all up the ladder, the woman passed the lantern to her husband, clapped her hands, and exclaimed, "Jade!" She ran over to the lounger, gauzy fabric flowing, reaching both arms out in greeting. "Elise has told us so much about you. How wonderful to have you here."

"Hi," Jade said. The word seemed hollow and thin next to Mrs. Parker's grand welcome.

It was quiet for an awkward moment before Mr. Parker said, "We're so thrilled Elise was able to talk your parents into letting you spend part of your summer with us." He turned to Aunt Elise. "How long have you been trying to get Jade here?"

"Since the day I left Philly."

"What made them decide this was the year?" Mrs. Parker asked.

Aunt Elise looked up to the deep purple sky. "The right set of circumstances, I guess."

Jade was grateful her aunt didn't elaborate on that right set of circumstances. She actually wondered how much her aunt knew about that morning, two Saturdays before, when her mom had been cleaning out the top shelf of Jade's closet and came across her "What I Did Over My Summer Vacation" papers. Jade didn't know what had possessed her to save them through the years. And worse, to put them into one binder so her mom could accidentally stumble across it and see what she had been writing every September, from Mrs. Minshew's first grade all the way through Miss Maybury's sixth grade last year.

But she guessed Aunt Elise knew something about it because, twenty-four hours after that discovery, Jade was presented with a round-trip plane ticket to Wyoming and a promise of *real* adventure. What Jade's mom didn't understand, however, was the fact that Jade liked her Philadelphia summers. She made up stories for those assignments because it was easier than standing in front of the class and admitting she had spent another summer watching *Addams Family* marathons on TV Land or writing the city council about when they were going to get off their rumps and enforce the No Skateboards on City Sidewalks ordinance. The rule had been on the books forever but no one cared about it because politicians rode around in their fancy cars with their drivers and never actually had the pleasure of getting mowed down by Phillip Turnbill or Chase Saunders.

Aunt Elise looked over to Jade and smiled, bright as the stars above. "I guess they figured twelve was old enough to strike out and have an adventure."

Mr. Parker smacked a hand on Aunt Elise's back. "We're all grateful for it, too. Isn't that right, Joshua?"

Roy twisted in his cowboy boots. "Dad! I told you to call me Roy."

"Oh, right. I sometimes forget that one. Isn't that right"—he paused and took a deep breath before finishing—"Roy?"

Roy looked thoroughly dejected. "Yes," he mumbled.

Now it was Jade's turn to give Roy the stink eye. What was he up to?

The adults clustered around a telescope off in one corner and Roy took Aunt Elise's lounger next to Jade.

"Hey, Joshua," she said, trying not to laugh.

"Very funny."

"Why the fake name?" It was surprisingly easy to talk

to someone while lying on your back in the dark. No face-to-face pressure.

"It's not fake. They would have named me Roy if they had known our heritage. They settled for Joshua because they didn't have all the facts."

"And now you've enlightened them?"

"That's right. I'll make it legal when I'm old enough. In the meantime, it's what I go by."

"Like a nickname?" Jade asked.

"I guess, though I'd consider it more than that. We have the same last name and I can feel Butch's blood running through my veins. Some days he seems so close I swear he's right with me. Like an angel."

"An outlaw angel, now that's a concept."

Roy's voice grew tense and hard. "Butch Cassidy was the Robin Hood of the West. He was a hero!"

Mrs. Parker turned from the telescope. "Go easy on her, son. Poor Jade doesn't understand your unusual interest in that old-time cowboy."

"He's not just an old cowboy, Mom, and it's not unusual to want to know about where you come from."

Mrs. Parker flicked a thin hand in the air. "Whatever you say, dear."

"That's right," Jade said, once the adults were busy chatting again. "I only know about how old Butch stole people's hard-earned money from banks and held up stage coaches full of innocent passengers." The truth was, Jade had known next to nothing about Butch Cassidy before Googling him that afternoon on Aunt Elise's computer and asking her mom about it when she called home to let her parents know she had arrived safely. She remembered her dad watching a movie by the same title and her mom explaining how Butch was a long-ago cowboy. After Roy's wisecrack about her not knowing what stars were, she figured she should be better prepared. "That's why he went by a fake name," she continued, reciting information from *Wikipedia*. "Because he was a crook. Still, if you say that's being a hero and you're related to him, I guess I won't argue."

Jade was half teasing so it surprised her to hear the quiver in Roy's voice when he responded. "Soon enough I'll have proof he's my great-great-uncle, for you and everyone else who doubts me. For your information, Jade"—he got all snotty on the *Jade* part—"I'm saving up to get my full genealogy."

Jade could see on Roy's face the pain she had caused him. "One thing you should know about me is that I'm lousy with jokes. I think I'm being funny, but I usually get it all jumbled up and wrong."

Roy's expression relaxed. "So that was your idea of a joke?"

"Sort of," Jade said.

"And you don't think Butch Cassidy hurt people? Because he didn't, you know. Can I tell you a true story?"

Jade shrugged. "Go for it."

"All right," Roy began. "One time Butch was passing by a ranch outside Heber City, Utah. By chance, he happened to have a satchel full of cash."

"How'd he get that cash?"

"Just listen, will you?"

"Fine," Jade said. "Continue."

Roy settled into his lounger. "He was tired so he asked the poor widow woman who owned the place if he could stay there for the night. She kindly obliged. In the morning, over breakfast, she told Butch he was lucky he'd come the night before because later that very morning, the banker was coming to take her ranch. She couldn't afford the back taxes and was about to lose it all. Can you guess what Butch did?"

"I have a feeling you're going to tell me."

"Dang straight, I am. He went to his satchel, pulled out that cash, and gave it to the woman. Just gave it to her!"

Jade had to admit she was impressed.

"Now the best part is still to come. Butch, being smart, left the ranch. He hid out in the brush, waiting for the banker to come along. Well, the banker man came, the

31

widow paid him off, and then Butch jumped out and robbed the banker soon as he cleared the property. Whoeee!" Roy swung his arm in the air. "He done secured that woman's land and kept his loot in the process!"

"But the bank lost their money," Jade said.

"Who cares about the stupid bank? They've got tons of cash and those taxes nearly crushed the poor homestead ranchers."

"Interesting," Jade said, not wanting to argue. "How do you know so much about Butch Cassidy?"

Roy turned back toward the winking heavens. "When I was in kindergarten, my teacher read a book about him to the class. I would watch the clock every morning, waiting for story hour to come. Then we'd all sit on the carpet in a half circle as she settled into her big blue chair in the corner and read another chapter. I suppose that's when I first wondered if there could be a real connection. Over the years, I've made it a point to learn as much as I could. Then for spring break this past April, I talked my parents into driving me to the town of Cody to visit Butch's Hole in the Wall Cabin. That's the famous hideout he and his gang used when they were on the run from the law. I tell you, when I stepped across that threshold it was like I was coming home, and I decided right then and there to take his name as my own." Then his voice got all wistful. "Now can you see how Butch Cassidy was a real hero?"

"If you say so, I believe it."

Roy smiled under the stars. "I say so."

They stayed up on the roof deep into the night, taking turns peering through the telescope and counting the shooting stars, which Aunt Elise said were not stars at all, but meteorites. "Meteorites are ice and rocks smashing into the Earth's atmosphere," she explained. They were tiny smears of light flashing through the blue-black sky and, by Jade's count, they had seen fourteen.

Mrs. Parker floated across the rooftop deck, pointing out constellations and chattering on about how Mr. Parker had spent the day pouring a concrete wheelchair ramp for someone named Angelo.

"What was that you were talking about earlier, when you said I came just in time?" Jade asked Roy.

Roy glanced over to the adults and shook his head. "When we're alone."

"It better be more than looking at some pregnant cow."

"Don't worry," Roy assured her. "It's more." There was a shadow of something outlining his words.

Aunt Elise suggested they call it a night and everyone gathered around the edge of the rooftop.

"How high are we?" Jade was looking at the driveway below.

"Are you afraid of heights?" Mrs. Parker asked.

"Not exactly," Jade said, "but I've never stepped backward off a roof onto a ladder before."

"It can feel intimidating at first," Aunt Elise said. "Take it one step at a time."

Mr. Parker gave a few pats to his round belly. "Let me go first. That way you'll have something soft to land on should you fall."

Jade couldn't help but smile. Still, the thought of turning around and stepping blindly off her aunt's roof in the pitch-black night had her feet feeling like worthless lumps of granite.

"Like it or not, you've got to do it," Roy said matter-of-factly. "You can't spend your whole vacation on this rooftop."

"You're right, Roy," Jade said.

"Then let's go." He walked over and stepped down first.

His parents followed, leaving Aunt Elise and Jade alone at the top. "Look right here," Aunt Elise said, lifting the lantern and pointing to her face. "The whole time you're taking that first step, hold on to these rails, feel with your foot, and keep your eyes on me."

Jade wiped her sweaty palms along the sides of her jeans and took a long, slow breath. She did like she was told, feeling with her foot and keeping her eyes focused on Aunt Elise's face. She noticed how her aunt's smile pushed her cheeks up into her bottom eyelashes and how the lantern light made her teeth gleam. She focused intently on the brown lines of pencil that made up most of her aunt's eyebrows and soon she realized she was halfway down the ladder.

"Chin up," Aunt Elise said. "Keep your focus on me." She was leaning over from the rooftop, smiling in a yellow circle of light. From where she was, Jade thought the image wasn't unlike those patron-saint pictures she had seen with the golden halos framing each divine head. Saint Elise, guardian of the ladder descenders.

And then Jade's foot hit the ground.

"Huzzah!" Mr. Parker punched a fist into the night.

Aunt Elise was down in a flash. "You were so brave—exactly like Robinson Crusoe in that moment." She was beaming at Jade's side. "In that scene where he saw the eyes of a devil in the cave and decided to confront his fear face-to-face."

A muddle of relief and elation was pulsing through Jade's veins. "I read that part. He was freaking out, but when he went inside the cave, it was only a goat."

"Exactly." Aunt Elise gave a pat to the side of the ladder. "Tonight, my fellow adventurer, you turned this devil into a goat."

"It will get easier from here on out," Mr. Parker promised.

"Not bad for a city girl," Roy added.

"Let's head home," Mr. Parker said.

"You were right about Jade," Mrs. Parker said. "She is something else." Then she took Roy by the hand and followed her husband down the driveway.

Aunt Elise turned to Jade. "You must be exhausted."

Jade *was* exhausted. Philadelphia time was two hours later than Wellington time so their midnight was her two in the morning. She followed Aunt Elise inside, went to her new room, and climbed into bed. The room was cozy enough, but it still wasn't *her* bedroom. It still wasn't home. She let out a ragged breath, thinking of her own blue-and-yellow bedspread and perfectly cushy pillows back home. More than anything, that was where she longed to be.

Rain started up again, pelting the windows and

clattering against the flat roof. Jade snuggled in and thought of what Aunt Elise had said about her being brave. There were a lot of words Jade would use to describe herself: smart, thoughtful, loyal, occasionally funny if she got it just right, prudent—that was a good one—but never brave and never ever anything close to adventurous.

Jade decided to read a few more pages in her book when a soft *purr* slid through the crack in the door and, a moment later, Copernicus bounded onto the bed. He circled around, working the quilt this way and that, nestling down to sleep.

Jade pulled her knees up away from the cat. "Go on," she said, "scat."

Copernicus positioned himself right in the middle of the bottom half of her bed and clearly had no intention of leaving. Jade jabbed at the cat with her foot, but he didn't move. She let out another tired breath and put the book on the side table. Then she turned out the light, curled up near the head of the bed, and decided to let him be. It was an interesting feeling to have another presence in the room—hearing the cat's smooth *purr* and feeling his weight on the covers. It reminded her of when she was a little girl, only three or four years old. How her mother used to sit at the foot of her bed and hum soft lullabies into the night. The music would weave its way through the darkness and ease her to sleep.

Somewhere along the way, though, she had become too old for lullabies and now it had been years since her mother tucked her in that way. Years since anything had hummed her to sleep.

5

Morning sun cut through a slit in the curtains. Jade blinked and rubbed her eyes awake. Copernicus reached out his front paws, stretched, and jumped off the bed. The pine-plank floors were cool under Jade's feet and the warm, salty smell of bacon pulled her toward the kitchen.

"Hello, Morning Glory," Aunt Elise sang out when Jade shuffled into the room.

Jade sat down at the table. "It smells wonderful. Thanks for cooking breakfast." She was used to cold cereal. Both her parents worked and were off before the sun even had a chance to think about rising.

"I wanted to make you bacon and eggs and pancakes but I hate washing a lot of dishes so I decided to try cooking them all in the same skillet." She was bustling around the stove and lobbing a black spatula in the air as she spoke.

Jade remembered dinner from the night before and started getting a sneaking impression her perfect breakfast was about to go down the tubes.

"It's all about improvisation." Aunt Elise slapped something onto a plate and ceremoniously turned to place it on the table. "Ta-da!"

Jade stared at her breakfast. It was a pancake with chunks of scrambled egg and pieces of bacon cooked right into the dough. An eddy of bacon grease lined the edges, seeping into the pancake and giving it a soggy sheen. "How creative," she said.

Aunt Elise was glowing. "I know! Don't be shy, there's plenty more where that came from."

Jade reached for the syrup and poured it over her breakfast conglomerate, trying to drown out the puddles of grease with sugar. The combination was tragic.

Aunt Elise sat down, resting her chin on both palms. "It's so great having you here!"

A tender feeling settled over the kitchen. It was the same feeling Jade had had when Astro sighed under her touch or when Copernicus peeked through one slit eye before falling asleep at her feet. It was warm and inviting. She took a fork and started picking at her plate. Aunt Elise danced back to the stove top and began jostling the batter bowl and pan.

"What's kickin', chicken?" Roy was at the back door. He sat down next to Jade and gave a twisted look at the mess of egg and meat and dough on her plate. He leaned over. "My mom's making cinnamon rolls over at our place. We can go there later if you want."

Jade shoved her fork into an egg glob. "I love this breakfast."

One side of Roy's mouth flattened out. "Suit yourself."

Jade took another bite, set down her fork, glanced over at her aunt, and whispered, "Maybe later."

"You want one, Roy?" Aunt Elise said from beside the stove. "I've got plenty."

"I'm good. Thanks, though." He leaned back in his chair and pulled his belt buckle up. This one was black with a bucking bronco carved into the metal. Jade noticed the saddle on the bronco was lined with red, white, and blue stones. "My mom sent me over because she said you might have a job for me today."

"Indeed I do," Aunt Elise said. "I was hoping you'd give the dogs a bath. I'll pay you five dollars a dog."

"I sure appreciate the work."

Aunt Elise waved the spatula at Jade. "Maybe you can convince this one to be your assistant."

Roy sat up. "I'd like the help, but I would have to pay Jade's portion in cinnamon rolls. I kind of need the cash right now."

"That's a decent offer," Aunt Elise said. "Nothing's better than Brenda's cinnamon rolls, except maybe her poetry."

"Your mom's a poet?" Jade asked.

"She messes with it, I guess."

"Help me with these dishes, why don't you, Jade," Aunt Elise suggested, "and then you can meet Roy out in the side yard by the dog runs."

Roy started toward the door. "But don't dawdle. I'm only offering our prize-winning cinnamon rolls for real work."

"Dawdle?" Jade asked.

"It's a Wyoming thing." And he was out the door.

Aunt Elise dropped the batter bowl into the sink and turned on the faucet. "That boy," she said, shaking her head. "What a character."

Jade was tempted to agree—Roy was funny. But he wasn't a character. It was clear he took the cowboy lifestyle seriously.

After wiping down the table and helping her aunt dry and put away the few dishes, Jade headed out to meet Roy. He was turning off the hose bib by an aluminum tub of soapy water.

"Perfect timing," he said. "You let them out of their

runs and I'll get a rope tied to this post so they can't take off during their bath."

Jade started opening the chain-link-fenced dog runs. Each run had a doghouse, food and water bowls, mounds of straw for lounging, and a single dog. Aunt Elise had told her the night before that the dogs were allowed to roam her fenced yard during the day, but went into their individual runs at night. Jade thought that was practical.

As she opened the gates, some dogs came running, hoping it was time for a morning stroll or treat. Others lay back in their piles of straw and offered up sorrowful looks like, *Do you not see me sleeping?*

Astro was one of the latter.

"Come on, boy," Jade called, waving a hand.

Astro couldn't care less about the open gate or theatrics. He raised his head, looked at Jade, and laid his head back down again. Decision made.

"You're going to have to go in and pull him out by the collar," Roy said.

Jade gave Roy a look. "He's happy where he is. I don't want to upset him."

"Go on. He's feeling lazy is all. Sometimes you gotta let them know who's boss."

Jade looked at the muscles rippling down Astro's back and thick neck. "I think we both know he's boss."

"Is that one of those failed-joke attempts again?" Roy asked, tying the last loop of the rope on the post.

Jade went into the dog run and reached toward Astro. "It's okay, boy. I'm here to help you." Astro pressed his head against Jade's outstretched hand, like he was asking for some love. "Aw, that's sweet." Jade scratched behind his ears and wrapped her fingers around his collar. "Let's come out and have a bath," she said, pulling on the collar.

Astro didn't move. Jade tugged and pulled but the dog wouldn't budge an inch. She dug her heels into the ground, leaned back, and yanked mightily. The collar slipped up, over, and off Astro's head, sending Jade into a backward lunge to the ground. *Thunk!*

Roy let out a deep belly laugh.

"I thought a real cowboy would always help a damsel in distress, not sit and laugh at her."

Roy adjusted his belt buckle. "You're right," he said, coming over and helping Jade off the ground. "It was just so funny to see you go flying through the air."

"Hilarious." Jade brushed the red clay dust from her bottom.

Roy reached into his pocket and pulled out a chunk of jerky. "This'll do the job," he said, waving the dried meat under Astro's nose and then walking over and tossing it on the grass. Astro came out of his run and collapsed onto the lawn.

"Get Lobo," Roy said. "We'll start with him."

Jade looked across the yard, where a gaggle of dogs were sniffing through the dewy grass. "Which one is Lobo?"

Roy whistled, bringing the dogs running. "Let me introduce you." He went through, touching each dog's head, scratching its ears and rubbing the spot between its eyes. "This one is Mia," he said, tugging on the collar of the white, jumpy dog. "She's a shepherd mix. Then there's Yaz here, he's a spaniel. Sadie and Lady come every few weeks when their mom goes away on business." He was pointing out two identical collies—both with long copper fur and white tufts around their noses and ears. "Emerson is a beagle. If you hear a dog howling, it's likely Emerson. Jack is a true mutt and proud of it. Astro needs no introduction."

"No," Jade said. "He took care of that himself."

"Astro will cure you of any shyness, like it or not." He lifted up a rolly black pug. "Isn't that right, Lobo?" The pug wiggled his stumpy tail and blinked his bug eyes. Three crooked teeth jutted from his bottom jaw over his upper lip.

Jade counted the dogs. "Wait, I thought there were nine."

"Ah," Roy said. "Genghis Khan, the terror of terriers." He raised his chin toward a run where the black-and-brown terrier had snuck back into his doghouse. "He doesn't like being told what to do."

"How do you know them all so well?"

"They're mostly return customers, especially in the summer when their owners travel more. Astro is always here, though. He's kind of their mascot, I guess." Roy set Lobo down in the tub and tied the rope around his collar. Shimmery soap bubbles rose up around the dog's face and Lobo began snapping his jaws, trying to eat them. With each bite, he'd lick his mouth and look confused, uncertain how the bubble had disappeared. Roy plunged his hands into the water and began running his fingers through Lobo's fur. Lobo closed his eyes and made grunting noises.

"I think he likes you." Jade sat down on the edge of the porch, feet dangling next to the big tub where Lobo was enjoying his bath.

"Of course he does." Roy offered his confident cowboy grin. "What's not to like?"

6

When the last clean dog was basking in the sun and Roy was hosing out the dirt at the bottom of the washtub, Jade once again brought up the subject she had been so curious about. "So, are you going to tell me what's going on?"

Roy turned off the hose, flipped the tub upside down against the side of the porch, and nodded. "I'll get my pay and we can talk on the way to my house for your cinnamon rolls." He went inside and then came out, folding a small stack of cash in half and shoving it into his pocket. "Let's go."

"How far is it?"

"Just down the road."

Jade followed him out onto the street. Bronze grass swayed and danced in the fields, dotted with pink coneflowers and purple wild-onion blossoms. A light breeze wrapped around them. Houses were sprawled out across the landscape, each at a polite distance from the next. Back in Philly, a house wasn't even allowed its own shadow.

"How big are these lots?"

"Anywhere from two to four acres. They're big enough to give people breathing room but still friendly enough to be a town." He pointed to a side yard where two shiny black horses were chewing on a pile of hay. "That's the best part of living here," he said. "The skies, the land, the people—they're all good. But the horses are something else."

"Have you ever owned one?" Jade asked.

"Nah," Roy said, "they don't come cheap. Someday I will, though." His words were full of faith.

Jade looked across the field where the horses nudged each other, each working to get the best clump of hay. "It seems real nice."

"For the most part," Roy agreed. "But some things are changing for the worse."

"Like what?"

"Well." Roy picked a purple onion blossom that was weaving out of a three-rail fence. It was a round purple fluff ball on a thin green stem. "It's a lot to tell; are you in a listening mood?"

Jade stopped and sat down on the curb. She motioned for Roy to join her. "Listening is what I do best of all."

Roy sat down and picked out one purple tuft after another from the onion blossom, shredding it by bits and pieces. "Okay," he started. "Wellington has always been a small town, a family town. My dad ran County Hardware, the local hardware store here, for the past fifteen years."

"Aunt Elise told me about the time your dad took her onto the roof to see stars."

"That's right," Roy said. "He has a way of knowing what people need, and he helped all sorts of folks with that store. If someone needed a tool, he'd give them a hands-on demonstration. If someone needed fencing, he'd go over to their house and help dig the holes for the posts. Heck, one time Mrs. Wilson brought in an actual lemon and had him match a gallon of paint to the fruit because she didn't think the paint chips were lemony enough." The memory of that made him laugh out loud.

"Your dad's a good guy."

"The best. He spent the past three days pouring a concrete wheelchair ramp for a friend of ours who used to be a coal miner and moved here a few years ago. Angelo has that awful black-lung disease and it's gotten worse lately. My dad didn't build the ramp because anyone asked him to—he did it because he happened to pass by when

Angelo was trying to maneuver his wheelchair up this rickety homemade dealy-o."

Jade remembered the mention of Angelo during stars the night before.

"Anyway, that hardware store was more than a job to my dad. It was part of who he was." The onion blossom was now just a stem so Roy started twisting it around his little finger.

"Was?"

"He had to close the doors two weeks ago. We aren't losing the lease until September first but he couldn't pay the electric bill and employees anymore." The flower stem was getting tight around Roy's pinkie.

Jade reached out and started gently unwinding the stem. "I'm sorry, Roy. That's got to be tough. Did your mom work at the store, too, or does she have another job?"

"She helped out when she could, especially these past few months."

"What about her poetry? Does she ever sell it?"

"Not really. The worst part is when you hear *why* we lost the business. This snake named Kip Farley moved into town last year and opened one of those ugly big-box home improvement stores four stoplights down from our place. And get this—it's called the Hammer and Nail. What kind of lame name is that?"

"Not terrible for a hardware store, actually."

"It's not a *store*, it's part of a heartless chain. Besides, whose side are you on?"

"Yours," Jade said.

"Good, because I think if we got another shot at it, you know, fought harder this time, we might be able to keep things going. People were blinded by the flashy signs and opening-day sales, but soon they'll see the service they get from my dad is worth more than a stupid bag of free popcorn or a ten-percent-off-gravel coupon. If we could get our hands on some cash, we could reopen the store and be back in the game."

"Couldn't your dad take out a loan?"

"He's done that already but the misers at the bank have cut him off. My parents used up most of their savings keeping it open these past six months. Now they're broke as a twenty-year-old mare. But that's all right, I've got a plan." He stood up and lifted his plaid shirttail, exposing a pistol shoved into his belt.

"Where'd you get that?" Jade asked in shock.

Roy pulled the pistol out of his waistband and tried to do a fancy trick of swinging it on his thumb, but the gun slipped from his hand and fell to the ground.

"Holy lizards, Roy!" Jade shouted. "You'll kill us both."

Roy reached down and picked the gun up. "Nah," he

said. "It looks real, but it's only pretend." He ran his fingers along the grooved handle. "My parents gave it to me for Christmas. It's a replica of a genuine Colt .45 Amnesty revolver. Exactly like the one Butch carried." He put it back into the waist of his jeans. "It has all the beauty of a real Colt, but it's hollow on the inside."

"It doesn't seem right for a kid to walk around with a pistol, real or not," Jade said.

Roy pointed down to the pavement and leaned in to Jade. "This here is the real West—wild as it gets. You stepped into cowboy territory when you got off that plane. Besides, I'm just having fun. I would never really harm anyone."

"I get it," Jade said. "So what's your big plan?"

"We're going to pull a Butch Cassidy." Roy kept his voice low and steady but Jade could hear the excitement pulsing right below the surface.

"*We*? Who is *we*?"

"You and me. Just like Butch and Sundance."

"Who is Sundance?"

Roy let out a moan and flung his arms to the side. "Are you serious?"

"Oh, I remember," Jade said, thinking back to the *Wikipedia* article she had read. "The Sundance Kid was Butch's sidekick."

"And guess where he was from, originally?"

Jade hadn't a clue.

"Pennsylvania."

"You're lying," Jade said.

"I am not. He wasn't from Philly like you are, but he was born in Phoenixville, Pennsylvania, with the name Harry Longabaugh. When he was fifteen, he hopped a wagon train to Wyoming, hooked up with Butch, and the rest is history. You can't tell me that it isn't more than just a coincidence . . . having you come here from Pennsylvania."

"It is just a coincidence, Roy."

"Well, it's perfect for my plan."

"What brilliant plan will get us the kind of money you need?"

"It's not for me, it's for my parents."

"Fess up," Jade said.

A smile played on Roy's lips. His eyes danced. His left boot started tapping on the asphalt.

"Come on, Roy, spit it out."

Roy nodded, hooked his gaze on Jade, and said, "You and me are gonna rob a bank."

7

Jade! What a surprise," Mrs. Parker said as Jade and Roy came up the steps. She swung the door open as if the people at Publishers Clearing House had landed on her front porch. "Wonderful to see you!"

Jade stepped inside. Velvety jazz music and the scent of sweet, warm yeast poured out from the kitchen. Jade's stomach grumbled, a reminder that she hadn't eaten more than a few bites of Aunt Elise's disastrous meals since she'd arrived the day before.

"I promised her some of your cinnamon rolls," Roy said, "as payment for helping me wash Elise's dogs."

"Ah," Mrs. Parker said. "You absolutely must try one hot from the oven."

Jade wasn't about to argue. She followed Roy and Mrs. Parker into the kitchen, where the luscious smell tripled in strength and mingled with hints of cinnamon and butter.

"Where's Dad?" Roy asked.

"He's finishing up at Angelo's today. I'm sure he'd appreciate a helping hand if you two are free." Mrs. Parker placed rolls onto two plates and set them on the table. "You can take some for Angelo and Tilly, too."

Jade looked down at her plate. Buttery, moist cinnamon swirled through the roll and white frosting eased down the sides.

"Eat up, Kid," Roy said with a wink. It was his way of reminding Jade of his plan to rob a bank. His ridiculous, ludicrous plan.

"I told you I'm not doing it, Roy. And neither are you."

"What are you two whispering about?" Mrs. Parker was flitting and floating around the kitchen, swaying to the music pouring out from a corner iPod station. Her yellow skirt billowed with each turn of her hips.

"We're talking about the adventures we're going to have this summer," Roy said.

"Ah," Mrs. Parker said, "'the tragical To-be.'" She swiveled and bobbed to the beat.

"That's from Thomas Hardy's poem 'Embarcation,'" Roy said, like it was common knowledge.

"The beginning of an unknown," Mrs. Parker added. "The precipice of adventure."

"Precipice." Jade let the word roll over her tongue and scrape the roof of her mouth. "What's the definition?"

"It means a very steep cliff or falling-off point," Mrs. Parker said.

"That's not what we were talking about at all." Jade looked at Roy pointedly.

"We'll see," Roy said.

Jade pushed the side of her fork down to cut the cinnamon roll, uncovering more of the glass plate underneath. It was uneven and slightly less than round, but the cobalt-blue color was stunning. "This is a gorgeous plate, Mrs. Parker."

"Do you like it?" She placed a glass of milk down in front of Jade. The glass was twisted and somewhat misshapen but the color was that easy green of early spring leaves. "William made these pieces."

Jade turned to Roy. "Your dad made these?"

"You should have Roy show you his workshop out in the garage," Mrs. Parker continued. "It's a jumble of ingenuity out there."

"Jumble of ingenuity," Jade said. "That's a great phrase." She took a swig of milk and set the glass down. "One time my parents took me to a glass exhibit in Philly and, as pretty as those pieces were, they weren't this beautiful. How would you describe these colors? Vibrant? Vivid? Luminous?"

"You two and your words," Roy said through a mouthful of dough. "What he should *really* do is sell his kiln so we can reopen the hardware store."

"Now, Roy, don't get started on that again." Mrs. Parker quit her flitting and stood with her hands on her narrow hips. "Your father is allowed some joy in this life."

"The store brought him joy," Roy said. "Helping people all day long."

"That's true," Mrs. Parker said, "but you can't expect him to walk away from his glasswork. 'Art is heart,'" she quoted.

"Who wrote that?" Jade asked.

Mrs. Parker stood up straight. "Me."

Roy rolled his eyes. "I'm not asking him to stop forever. Just until we can get on top of things."

"How many cinnamon rolls did he promise you?" Mrs. Parker asked Jade, clearly anxious to change the subject.

"We didn't talk numbers."

"Will half a dozen do?"

"Oh yes, thank you," Jade said. Six of the oversize, gooey rolls would nicely supplement Aunt Elise's cooking.

"I'll throw in one more for good measure." Mrs. Parker

put the rolls into a plastic bag and tied it closed with a strip of pink ribbon. Then she was back to twirling. Sunlight cut through the mini-blinds, laying horizontal lines of light across the tile floor, and she danced across those lines like she was playing a piano with her toes.

8

After finishing their second cinnamon rolls, Jade and Roy headed off to help Roy's dad. Mrs. Parker sent more rolls with them on a sunshine-yellow glass plate. "Tell Angelo and Tilly I said hello," she said.

As Jade walked, she enjoyed the simple beauty of the wide, breezy fields and stark mountain ranges of Wyoming. It was unassuming and comfortable like her soft leather sandals.

When they turned the corner at the stop sign, Jade saw Mr. Parker immediately. He was removing plywood sheets from the side of a new wheelchair ramp going from the driveway up to the front door of a bright pink house. A brawny man with a long white beard, shaggy mustache, and broad shoulders sat in a rocker on the porch. He didn't look like someone who would live in a pink house. As soon as Mr. Parker saw Roy and Jade, he stopped working and came over. "I could almost smell Brenda's cinnamon rolls from all the way around the corner. Your timing is impeccable."

"I love your glasswork," Jade said. "This yellow is so cheerful."

"Thank you, my dear," Mr. Parker said. "It's all about getting the right frit."

"What's frit?" Jade asked.

Roy answered, "It's a special colored powder you roll the clear glass in as you form it. And the good stuff is . . ." He let out a whistle that must have meant *pretty expensive.*

"You can also start with colored rods," Mr. Parker offered. "That costs less."

"Sometimes it's worth getting the good stuff," the bearded man said from his rocking chair. His voice was like rocks tumbling down a mountainside—sharp and choppy and broken. "When you're as good as William is." Then he launched into a coughing fit. When he finished, his rocker was swaying and he was wiping a hand down his beard. "Sorry about that," the man said.

Roy leaned into Jade. "That's his black-lung disease,"

he whispered. Then, in a regular voice, he said, "Angelo was a coal miner over in Campbell County."

"Worked the mines for thirty-seven years," Angelo said. He rolled his rocking chair forward and dipped his head. "Pleased to meet you."

"I'm Jade."

"I know," Angelo said, rolling back in his chair. "Roy has done nothing but talk about your visit. Jade Landers, age twelve, city girl from Philadelphia, and partner in crime for the summer."

"He's kidding," Jade assured him. "There won't be any actual crime going on." Her voice was tight.

Angelo laughed at that, which started another coughing fit.

"We came to help with the ramp," Roy said to his dad.

Mr. Parker swung an arm out wide. "I'm just finishing up. Isn't it a beauty?"

"Let's give it a whirl," Angelo said. Then he called, "Tilly!" His voice cracked in the middle of the word.

An old woman came to the door. She was weatherworn, sienna brown, and had gray curls springing out from every direction on her head. She wore a pink housedress, pink flip-flops, and had bubblegum-pink nail polish on her fingers and toes. Jade suddenly understood the house color.

"You must be Elise's niece," Tilly said. "Welcome to Wellington."

"Thanks," Jade said, shaking her hand.

"Can you bring out that blasted wheelchair?" Angelo asked.

Tilly went back inside and came out with the chair. She positioned it right next to Angelo's rocker.

Tilly settled her husband in, jumped behind the chair, and started pushing it forward.

"Stop that!" Angelo waved a hand behind his head. "I can do it myself."

"Having to use this thing has been so difficult for Angelo," Tilly explained apologetically. "It's hard for him to be slowed down."

"Quit talking about me like I'm not even here," Angelo grumped. "I'm right here!"

Tilly put her pink-polished fingernails on his shoulder. "Cantankerous old goat."

Angelo smiled at that.

Mr. Parker pulled out the last two-by-four from the side of the ramp. "I think it's ready for an inaugural run."

Angelo maneuvered across the porch and onto the ramp. With one solid push, he went sailing down, arms raised up high like he was on the Coney Island Cyclone.

Both Tilly and Mr. Parker went running after him, grabbing his wheelchair as it spun out onto the driveway.

"You'll kill yourself doing that!" Tilly said. "Crazy fool."

Angelo looked back at the ramp. "Yep," he said. "It'll do fine."

9

Jade found her aunt sitting on the front steps the following morning. Cotton-ball thunderheads galloped across the sky, casting dark, round shadows on the land. Astro led the band of dogs onto the porch as the first fat raindrops pattered into the red, dusty earth.

"There wasn't a cloud in the sky yesterday," Jade said.

"Weather is moody out here."

"Will this be like the storm we hit coming home from the airport?"

Aunt Elise leaned out from under the porch and peered up at the clouds. "Nope," she said. "This is the kind that likes to puff around making a lot of noise, but looks worse than it is."

Jade looked up, too. She couldn't tell the difference

between these clouds and the ones that had nearly fried them with lightning two days before. "How do you know?"

Aunt Elise pulled Lobo onto her lap. "I just do. These clouds will give us some rain, but their bark is worse than their bite, isn't that right, Lobo?" The pug wiggled and blinked his bug eyes. "What are your grand plans for today?"

"Roy asked me to come over when I could."

"I've never met a better bunch of people than the Parkers."

"It's too bad about them losing their business."

Sadie and Lady, the twin collies, came over to Aunt Elise. She pushed her fingers into their long fur and gave them each a good scratch. "Roy told you about that?"

"He's kind of obsessed with it."

"Well," Aunt Elise said, "his family is in a tough spot right now." She rearranged Lobo on her lap. He grunted and snorted and rested his chin on her knee, closing his eyes.

"I know." Jade considered telling her aunt about Roy's master plan, but let it go. It wasn't like it was ever going to happen, so it seemed pointless to rat him out.

"I try to offer Roy a job or two when I can think of any. It's not enough to reopen the store or pay off their debt, but I hope it helps him have spending money of his own."

"I'm sure it helps," Jade said.

Aunt Elise ran a hand along Lobo's back. "Mostly it's to make them feel supported. I think you need friends to rally around you at a time like this."

"I remember when a girl from my school got sick and had to have an operation. Our neighborhood had a huge yard sale to raise money for her bills."

"That's an idea."

Broad haphazard raindrops kept splattering across the yard. Jade sat down on the bench under the living room window. Astro came up and collapsed across her flip-flops, pinning her feet to the floorboards of the porch. The weight was comforting.

Sitting there, Jade began thinking about Wyoming's remarkable kaleidoscope skies and had an idea. "What about teaching astronomy classes on your roof?" she said, her words bouncing with excitement. "You could advertise all around town. It could be a fund-raiser for the Parkers."

Aunt Elise scoffed, "Folks 'round here see the stars every night. No need to pay me for it."

"You're the one who showed me how it's not the same view from the ground. You could teach merit-badge classes or host a couples' romantic night or birthday parties. Not everyone has a telescope. Most of the houses I've seen around here don't even have flat roofs."

Jade could see the idea rolling across her aunt's mind. "I do like the thought of being a teacher, but I wouldn't want to make William feel like a charity project."

"We won't tell him why we're holding the classes. We can save up the money and give it to him as a gift."

"It's not a bad idea, actually," Aunt Elise said. "Maybe I can whip up some snacks to serve, too." Jade didn't mean to make a face, but she must have because her aunt laughed and said, "All right, we'll appoint you as executive chef."

"Me?"

"Why not? You said you liked to watch the Food Network and, to be quite honest, anything you make is bound to taste better than my cooking."

"I guess I can try." Jade was getting more excited. "How about you print up some flyers and I'll take them around. We could even run an advertisement in the online classifieds for the local paper. How much do you think we should charge? Twenty dollars a ticket?"

"People might pay money like that in Philadelphia, but it seems a tad steep for this area."

"Fine," Jade said. "We'll charge fifteen." The minute those words flew off her tongue, she started doing the math. Fifteen dollars per person meant Aunt Elise would earn fifteen hundred dollars with only a hundred students. She didn't know how much Mr. Parker needed to reopen his store, but those numbers sounded promising.

Aunt Elise stood up and walked out to the edge of the porch, watching the rain spurt and spatter across the dusty earth. From this spot, they could see beyond the houses to the Teton mountain range off at the edge of the horizon. Jade never knew mountains could be so rough.

"You've climbed that big one seventeen times?" Jade asked.

Aunt Elise kept her gaze out to the world before them. "To the top," she said.

Jade studied the strong, harsh rocks of the mountain range. "It looks like a bunch of skeleton fingers coming up out of the earth and clawing at the sky."

Aunt Elise turned back to Jade. "It has to be that way." Her words were sure. "If the mountain was smooth, you wouldn't be able to climb it."

10

Jade bounded over to Roy's house as soon as the rain stopped. She was dying to tell him about her plan to have Aunt Elise teach astronomy classes as a way to help his family. She knew it wouldn't fix the whole problem, but maybe—if they all pitched in—they could help the Parkers get back on their feet.

As she approached the house, she heard jazz music coming from Mr. Parker's workshop. Only it wasn't the perky, light music Mrs. Parker had been dancing to in the kitchen. This jazz riff was entirely different—slow and lingering and dripping with heartache. The door was slightly ajar, so Jade peeked in.

Mr. Parker was sitting on a red vinyl bar stool. He was leaning against a huge metal box, his eyes closed and his fingers grazing against the metal in a drumming pattern.

There was a sadness to that beat that vibrated deep in Jade's bones. *Thrum, drum, thrum.* She had never seen a glass kiln before, but she guessed that was what Mr. Parker was leaning against. The one Roy said he should sell.

Jade began to step away from the door just as Mr. Parker stopped thrumming and looked up.

"Jade," he said, pulling his rectangular glasses from the pocket of his ragged brown bathrobe. "It's nice to see you." His hair frizzled out from his head like rays from the sun.

"Sorry to interrupt."

"A friend is never an interruption." Mr. Parker ran his foot along the bottom rung of the bar stool. "I was out here thinking." His words were soft and wistful and he kept his head down for a stretched-out minute before looking up with a warm smile. "Roy'll be glad to see you. Feel free to go on inside."

Jade left the workshop door, shaking off the sad notes of that jazz song and reminding herself of the reason she had come. Of the good news she had to share. She found Roy on their front steps. "He was out there all night," Roy said, knowing Jade had come from the workshop. "How'd he look?"

"Miserable." Jade sat down next to Roy.

"It's my fault. I got on his case again about selling his glassblowing equipment so we could reopen County

Hardware." He pulled at tufts of grass pushing up through a crack in the concrete. "I think I went too far this time."

"Why don't you tell him you were wrong and that you want him to keep it after all?"

Roy sucked in a slow, deep breath and eased it out. "I should," he said. "I *know* I should. But between the kiln and the annealer—not to mention all of his tools—he's probably got ten thousand dollars worth of stuff in there."

Jade guessed ten thousand dollars would go pretty far toward helping the family out.

"Part of me wants him to sell it and the other part is afraid if he *does* sell it, I'll feel like pond scum for the rest of my life." He went back to picking at the grass.

"I have a plan to make some money."

Roy's head popped up. "Go on."

Jade spelled out how Aunt Elise was going to teach classes and how she was going to try to bake treats. "At fifteen dollars a person, we'd only need three hundred and thirty-five students to make over five thousand dollars!"

"You did that math in your head?"

"I'm pretty good at numbers."

"Good," Roy said, "run these. How many people do you think will fit on top of Elise's roof?"

"Twenty at a time," Jade said.

"Try ten. It's small and, even though there's a ledge,

you still need to be careful. Dead students don't pay their bills."

"Fine. Ten it is. Aunt Elise is going to print up the flyers and make us a list of where I can drop them off all over Wellington. You can help me take them around."

"Hold your horses," Roy said. "Let's figure this out. Say you're able to book one class a week. That's ten students times fifteen dollars times four days a month . . ."

"That's six hundred dollars a month!"

"You are good at numbers," Roy said. "Now, how many months does Wyoming have fair weather?"

Jade hadn't considered the weather. "I don't know."

"I do," Roy said. "It's five. Five months out of the year when we don't have snow or ice. That's not accounting for the summer storms. They can be pretty bad and, at the start of summer, it rains quite a bit. No one will be standing on the roof looking at the sky if it's pouring outside. Count those in as one weekend a month, for safety's sake. What does that give us?"

Jade worked the math. "One hundred and fifty dollars times three lessons a month times five months out of the year . . ."

Roy finished her thought. "I count that in the neighborhood of twenty-two hundred dollars. And that's after a whole year! We have until September first before our lease ends and the owner rents the space to some other business. Not even two lousy months!"

Jade knew Roy was right. "But Aunt Elise was so excited about teaching the classes."

"Have her do it. It'll help some and, along with my plans . . ."

"I told you, Roy, I am not robbing a bank!"

"Who knows what we'll do," Roy said. "But either way, I'm full of ideas. You see, I was exploring Farley's ranch just before sunrise this morning."

"Spying?"

"Let's call it reconnaissance. He had this sign up on his front gate saying he was looking for ranch hands."

Jade's eyes went wide. "You want to work for Farley? What kind of pay is he offering?"

"It's not about the pay," Roy said, "though that would be a bonus. It's about getting inside his place and continuing our investigation and maybe even working some Butch Cassidy magic in the process."

Jade lost her breath. "Are you suggesting we steal from him? That's insane!"

"Did Robin Hood *steal*, Jade?"

"Yes!"

Roy slumped down, put his hands over his face, and let out a frustrated moan. "You don't get it," he said. "Kip

Farley is the thief. He comes into town with his neon signs, double-wide parking spaces, and patio furniture at ridiculously low prices and little by little steals the heart and soul out of the town we love." Roy tempered his voice, making it steady and strong. "It is exactly like the big cattle barons back in Butch's day that came in and did everything they could to squeeze the lifeblood out of the local ranchers. Farley is like the railroads and cattle companies and crooked politicians. We might as well be living in 1885! And do you know what Butch did to those cattle ranchers? He went to work for them. He learned how they operated, what their secrets were. Then he swiped the cattle right out from under their noses."

"It's a bad idea, Roy. Kip Farley doesn't have any secrets. He's probably just a regular guy who happened to open a big business in a small town."

"Don't be so naïve. There must be some way to bring him down, or at least shake up his business enough to give our store another shot." He stood up. "I'm going in."

11

Kip Farley's house sat behind a tall wooden fence. Jade could see the Spanish-tile roof poking over the top, but everything else was hidden behind those beige pine slats.

"Last chance to change your mind," Jade said as they stood at the main gate.

Roy shook his head. "We're just going to talk to him, see what kind of work he needs done."

"No way." Jade stepped back. "*You're* going to talk to him. I'm only here for moral support."

Roy walked to the edge of the gate, peered between two slats, stepped back, and then turned and walked to the opposite edge.

He had been doing that for twenty minutes: pacing, peering, pacing.

"Come on," Jade said, "let's go home."

"I told you I'm going in."

"Sure you are."

Roy went back to pacing. Jade sat on the curb and thought about Philly. How she might have gone to Franklin Square with her friends by now, or had banana milk shakes with her parents at Nifty Fifty's. She looked up at Roy. "We've been sitting here forever. You're not going anywhere near that house and we both know it."

That did it. Roy clamped down his jaw, reached out, and opened the gate.

There was a curved brick path leading up to the house. At the top of the path was a rottweiler, tied to a porch rail with a rope. As Jade and Roy stepped through the gate, the dog went berserk, pulling at his rope and exploding into a fit of barking teeth.

All of which brought Kip Farley to his front door.

Jade pulled Roy back. "Let's get out of here."

Roy shook off her grip and walked forward. Jade followed, trying to pretend the dog wasn't even there. The blood was hammering through her veins. Every inch of her skin felt prickly, but she forced her feet to press forward. It took everything she had. As they neared the front porch, Kip Farley looked at the dog and said, "Quiet." The dog snapped his mouth shut and dropped down on the red-tiled floor of the porch.

Roy extended his hand and said, "Roy Parker. This here is my friend Jade. She's new to Wellington."

Looking at Kip Farley, Jade decided he was everything she expected from Wyoming. Tall and broad, wearing a wide Stetson hat and a proper bolo tie. His eyes were like blue silk and his smile was smooth as polished marble.

"I'm Elise Bennett's niece and I'm just visiting," Jade corrected.

Kip Farley shook Roy's hand and then reached out to Jade, taking her hand in his two strong palms, sandwich-like. "It's a pleasure to meet you, Just Visiting." There was an easiness about him that surprised Jade, a warm hospitality that stood in stark contrast to the tall fence and fierce rottweiler.

"We saw your sign about needing ranch hands and came to apply," Roy said.

Kip Farley tilted his head. "A bit young to be looking for work, aren't you?"

"Twelve is old enough and we're good workers."

Kip leaned sideways, toward Jade. "This little cowboy's all business, isn't he?"

She folded her arms. "I told him we shouldn't come."

Kip Farley worked his fingers through a ring of keys hanging from his belt loop. They *clink-clinked* against each other like ice cubes in a glass. "No, no. I'm glad you did. Good workers are hard to find and I've never been one to hold a man's age against him."

"What's the work and when can we start?" Roy asked.

"There's no need to rush headlong into those discussions. Why don't we take a load off and wet our whistles before we get into that bag of nails." His cowboy talk rolled off his tongue in waves and lilts.

Roy looked so proud you would have thought he'd been crowned rodeo king.

"We're not thirsty," Jade said.

"You got root beer?" Roy asked.

Kip Farley's smile widened. "I got whatever you need." He placed a hand on Roy's back and started ushering him into the house.

"He'll take it out here," Jade piped in. "On the porch." She pulled Roy over to her side.

"All right, I see who's in charge," Kip Farley said. He called out "Anita!" and an old woman in an apron came to the door. "One root beer," he requested. The woman nodded and disappeared into the shadows behind the screen. A moment later, she reappeared with a dark brown bottle on a tray. She set the tray down on a side table and went back inside. Roy wrapped his hand around that bottle and eyed it, then eased on a smile, and took a long drink.

"Real refreshment for a real cowboy," Farley said.

Roy pushed a shoulder back and raised his chin.

"The work I have around here is basic ranch care, but if you prove yourself I'd consider allowing you to work your way up to some horse wrangling. Are you interested?"

"Am I!"

Jade knew it was over. Wrangling horses was the one thing Joshua "Roy" Parker would never be able to resist. Whatever wrangling was.

"I'd like you to start the day after tomorrow, around ten in the morning." Then he turned to Jade. "Will you be joining him?"

"I'm only going to be here for a few weeks and I'm supposed to be helping my aunt over at her dog ranch, but I'd like to try."

"That's fine, you come when you can." Farley turned back to Roy. "It seems we have a deal."

"Yes, sir," Roy said, taking Farley's hand and working it up and down, up and down like he was pumping for oil. "It seems we do."

"I'll look forward to seeing you both, then." Farley tugged on his hat once more and went back inside.

Jade followed Roy down the walk.

"What was that?" she asked when the gate was shut behind them.

Roy shoved Jade's shoulder. "That was you spoiling a prime opportunity to look inside Farley's house. We were so close!"

"He gave me the creeps—all smooth and glossy with that deep voice, calling you a cowboy. I can't believe you fell for it."

"Excuse me, but I am a cowboy. Besides, you're forgetting that it's all part of my master plan. I got a paying job, another way into Farley's world, and a cold root beer to wet my whistle."

"What do you mean *another* way?"

"Even a city girl like you has to know there's more than one way to skin a cat. I'm playing Farley like a campfire fiddle." He moved his arms through the air like he was working a violin.

"I don't know. I somehow get the feeling that he's the one playing you."

"Are you kidding me?" Roy poked a thumb toward the fence. "That went precisely as I had planned. Now you've got to promise me you won't go shootin' your mouth off about us working for Farley."

"Why not?"

"Parents are nosy by nature and I need some space to work my magic. Do you promise?"

"I don't know if I can keep a secret like this."

"Come on, Jade. Open up to some real adventure."

The way Roy said the word *real* made Jade suspicious. "Why would you say that?"

"Trust me on this one," Roy said.

Jade shielded her eyes and looked up at the sun tucked behind thick, downy clouds. "I better head back to the dog ranch. Aunt Elise will be wondering where I am."

"Okay, but meet me in front of my house at one tomorrow," Roy said. "I've got to run some errands with my mom in the morning and then I want to show you a few things."

12

As she had promised, Jade met Roy at one. He led her through the twisted streets of Wellington and right up to what was left of his dad's store, County Hardware. It sat at the end of a long, narrow parking lot, next to the bright orange Harold's Hot Dog Shack. Something about the words *Summer is here! Pop in and get your pansies* swirling across the front window in blue-and-green paint made Jade sad. It reminded her of the time, in second grade, when she walked into Classic Skate for Randi Waterford's eighth-birthday party, only to find a wide and empty room. She had stood there trying to will the pink-and-white polka-dotted present to stop trembling in her hands as the pimply-faced teenager behind the counter told her mother the party had been the day before.

That was how this felt—like the Parkers' store was all dressed up for a party that wasn't going to happen.

"There was a time when this parking lot would get packed with cars. We'd put our vegetable starts and potting soil out there by the front doors in the spring and swap them for bags of salt and ice melt in the winter." It was like Roy was showing Jade around his bedroom, getting all sentimental about the shopping carts and chipped-up paint on the front curb.

When they were standing in front of an electronic keypad on the side of a sliding metal door, Roy said, "Let's hope they haven't changed the code on us yet." He punched in six numbers, followed by the pound key. The door shuddered and started rolling up, *click, click, clacking* the whole way. When it jerked to a stop and the puffs of dust cleared from the air, Roy stepped inside. He stood in the middle of the storeroom, hands proudly on his hips, surveying the mostly empty shelves that lined the walls.

"Isn't it grand?"

Jade noticed two dusty toilets and a tower of bricks in the corner. "Sure."

"This isn't even the best part." Roy walked over and pushed a wide, swinging door open. Jade followed him into the main store area. Sun was streaming in the front windows, illuminating a blue-and-gold mosaic-tile pattern in the floor. Roy ran the point of his boot along the edge of one of the tiles. "My dad put this floor in all by himself." He walked over to a counter, which had two cash registers. "And we replaced this countertop last year—I got to pick out the stone. See how it has these gold flecks in it? The building owner let us do whatever improvements we wanted. It was like our own place."

Jade patted the countertop. "It's real nice, Roy."

He turned, leaned his back against the counter, and looked out across the expanse of the room. To Jade it looked like old shelves half-spotted with boxes and clearance signs but she knew it looked like paradise to Roy.

"Did I ever tell you about what happened to Butch Cassidy when he was a little older than us—only thirteen years old?"

"You know?" It was a silly question. Of course he knew.

"He went by the name Roy back then and his family lived in Beaver, Utah. One day, he rode into town to talk to the shop owner about buying some overalls. He was hoping to strike a good bargain. When he got to the general store, it was closed. He could have come back another day, but it was a long ride into town and he was kept pretty busy on his family's ranch. So he decided to let himself in and leave a written IOU note in exchange for the pants. He left his real name and everything!"

"That sounds fair enough," Jade said, though she wondered what her local grocery store manager might think if she helped herself to a case of Oreo cookies and left an IOU note. Maybe he wouldn't mind, but she doubted it.

Roy went on. "When the store owner came in the next day, he saw the note and called the sheriff. Without even talking to Butch!"

"Who went by Roy at the time," Jade clarified.

"Right."

Jade shook her head.

"Back in those days, a person's word was their bond. Butch Cassidy never made a promise he didn't keep. He had every intention of coming back and working out a fair deal for those pants, but folks never gave him a chance to make it right. They wrote him off as some crazy thief and filed charges. They didn't even try to understand him. That was the beginning of it all for Butch."

Jade looked at Roy. He was hanging his head, staring down at the tips of his cowboy boots. She wondered how much that last part of the story fit the Roy standing next to her. "Thirteen is awfully young to be so misunderstood," she said.

"You know something?" Roy said. "I think you would have gotten along real well with Butch." Then his round cheeks spread out into a smile. "Care to walk four stoplights down the road with me?"

13

Jade knew where Roy was taking her, she just didn't understand why. After being shown around County Hardware and seeing how connected he was to that place, she couldn't imagine why he'd want to rub in the sight of their empty parking lot by contrasting it to Farley's busy store.

When they came upon the Hammer and Nail, Roy crossed the street and settled in behind the wide trunk of an old walnut tree. "Come on," he said with a jerk of his head.

Jade crossed and stepped up to his side. "What are we looking at?"

"Nothing from down here. There's too much risk we'll be seen." He grabbed a low branch, hooked the toe of his boot into a knothole, and began pulling himself up. The way he moved let Jade know he had made the climb before. Hand over head, sure and confident. When he reached a thick branch near the middle, he turned back. "You coming?"

"I'll watch from here."

"That's no fun. Come on up with me." He moved over and brushed his hand across the thick branch. "There's plenty of room." He had a teasing look in his eyes. "Unless you're afraid or something."

"I'm not afraid," Jade said. "It's just that we don't go around climbing enormous trees in Philly. It's dangerous. Besides, I'm pretty sure it's against city ordinance."

Roy looked surprised. "I never knew a person could live twelve whole years without ever climbing a tree." He got all determined. "You can do this, Jade Landers, and I'm the one to talk you through it. Grab the first branch and shove your foot into that big knothole."

"Fine," Jade said, tugging on the hem of her shorts and then reaching up for the low branch.

"Now take hold of that next one, off to the right."

Jade hauled herself up, following Roy's direction at each step. She was three full branches into the climb when her foot hit a patch of moss and slipped, sending her tumbling and crashing to the ground.

"Are you all right?" Roy asked from his perch.

Jade rolled over on her side, trying to find some air in her lungs. "I fell," she said.

"I saw that part."

Jade looked down and noticed dark red blood pushing up out of some torn skin on her kneecap.

"Is anything broken?"

"No."

"Well, are you just going to lie there and bleed?"

Jade was speechless. She sat up and brushed the hair away from her face. She took a cold, wet clump of leaves and gently pressed them to her burning, tattered knee. She paced her breaths. She ignored Roy.

"I said—" Roy began.

"I heard you," Jade snapped. "For your information, I'm hurting here!"

Roy tempered his voice. "Yes, I know. And you have a choice. You can sit there feeling sorry for yourself or you can cowboy up and climb this tree."

Frustration pulsed underneath Jade's skin and water rimmed her eyes. She sank her head into her hands and groaned. Her knee was searing with pain, but she knew Roy was right. It was only a medium-size scrape.

"A little sympathy wouldn't kill you," she said, standing up and returning to the base of the trunk. A trickle of blood ran down her shin.

"What do you mean? I asked you if anything was broken."

Jade grabbed on to the bottom branch and began working her way back up into the tree. She moved with more surety this time. Hands first, double-checking her footholds as she went, not looking down. Soon she was at Roy's side.

"I knew you had it in you."

"Thanks," Jade said. Looking out through the broad canopy of leaves, Jade could see a half-full parking lot and a cluster of people standing around the front of Farley's store. The sight of those people milling and chatting and gathering made her heart slump. "They must be having a big sale or something," she said. "It looks busy."

"Sure it is." Jade expected to hear some measure of sadness in Roy's voice, but it was as light as could be. "On the outside."

A couple of employees came out of the store dressed in their red Hammer and Nail aprons, joining those who were already in the parking lot. Jade noticed how they were pinching their noses or waving their hands in front of their faces.

"Ha!" Roy belted out a laugh and then quickly slapped his hand over his mouth.

Jade grabbed on to the branch. "Careful," she said. "You nearly knocked me off."

"Sorry, it's just so blasted funny." He was shaking his

head and muffling giggles. "Can you see the looks on their faces? That one store clerk looks like she's about to pass out."

The picture began to be clear for Jade. The employees were all standing outside, shaking their heads. Then she noticed the CLOSED sign.

"Something must smell real bad inside," she said.

"If slimy old fish heads smell bad, I'd say you're right."

"Roy, what did you do?"

"I seized an opportunity, that's all."

"Spill it."

"I was just going to show you the Hammer and Nail but after we left Farley's yesterday and you went back to the dog ranch, I was minding my own business, walking along behind the grocery store when I noticed a couple of stray cats gathered around the base of a Dumpster. Then I saw how one of them had a half-chewed fish head in its mouth. After some investigation, I discovered there was a whole bag of fish heads and guts inside that Dumpster. And I said to myself, Roy, this here is what Butch would call prime opportunity. I figured slimy fish heads and guts would only last a short time in this summer heat before they got really ripe. And I guessed customers wouldn't care as much about free popcorn or ten-percent-off tree planting if their shopping experience wasn't as—how shall I put it—inviting?"

"You're nuts!"

"I'm crafty." Roy was all smiles. "I cut the fish up in tiny pieces and hid it all over the store. Not only that, I split up their alarm clock display, tucked them behind different merchandise, and set the alarms to go off in five-minute intervals. So every five minutes, they've got to track down another hidden alarm."

"But you know they'll find the alarms, clean up the fish, and be back in business tomorrow."

"Not tomorrow. It's going to take a while to fix this mess. And I bet customers will be slow to return after having such a *pleasant* experience. It's like what old Butch said: if you hurt them through their pocketbooks, they'll holler louder than if you cut off both legs."

"You better hope you don't get caught. I bet they have cameras in that store."

"I wasn't born yesterday, Jade. I saw the cameras and worked around them. If they go back and watch the footage, I'll just look like a kid interested in curtain rods and PVC pipe. They won't be able to prove anything." He looked at his watch. "I'd love to stay and see more, but it'd be better if we weren't hanging around and there's one last place I want to show you."

14

That one last place was the Wells Fargo bank.

"Why are we here?"

"It's the easiest thing to rob a bank," Roy said in his matter-of-fact way. "You don't even have to say a word. We just put on a disguise, walk in, hand over a note, and make sure they get a peek at my Colt." He touched his belt where he kept his pistol. "The whole thing takes sixty seconds, tops."

"We'll end up in prison, Roy. They have alarms. And guards."

Roy looked at his watch. "Let me show you something." He led her around the side and through the front doors. Right inside the lobby was an empty chair. Roy tilted his head at the chair and looked across the foyer of the bank. "See that door on the far side? That's the break room.

Calvin goes in there from four to four-thirty. He has a Pepsi and reads his newspaper—every single afternoon. This chair here stays empty and the bank stays unprotected. Not that Calvin is much to worry about anyway."

"You know the guard?"

"Wellington is a small town. Besides, I've been casing the joint."

Jade guessed Roy had waited his whole life to say those words. "Don't they have a sub come in while he's gone?"

"This is the frontier. People are trusting, sometimes to the point of stupid. Follow me." Roy went out the front doors and around back again. He pointed to a tan box mounted on the wall. "This is their electrical box. The phone lines, which carry the alarm system, and those cameras you're so worried about, all come together here. Tell me, where's the lock on this box?"

Jade could see the hole in the box where the padlock was supposed to be but wasn't.

"Snip these wires," Roy said, "and we're good to go. The teller can hit her silent-alarm button all she wants. No one will be receiving any signal."

"Won't the alarm company be alerted once the wires are cut? They'll have to call the police."

"I've thought about that, too. I happen to know the Wellington Police get false-alarm notices all the time. It's fairly common. We'll use that fact to our advantage by sneaking over here two or three times the week before to trip these wires."

"How?"

"Simple. We open the box, unthread the phone wire, and then immediately reattach it. Each time we fiddle with the wires, the alarm company will get a loss of signal and call the police. They'll come, check it out, and see that everything is all right. The more we send those false alarms, the slower those good old boys will respond, see? We'll be lulling them into a false sense of security because they'll think it's faulty wiring."

Jade was surprised. "As much as I hate to admit it, it's a pretty good plan. But we're just kids. It'll never work."

Roy looked like Jade had slapped him in the face. "Being kids is the best part because no one will suspect us! You'll be outside doing the electrical work and I'll deal with the teller. We'll work up some disguise to make me look older. Stilts or something. They won't know what hit 'em. You need to get over this idea about it being a crime."

"It is a crime, Roy. A very big crime."

Roy leaned in, his voice all whispery. "We look at the law differently out here. The way I figure it, the bank is insured by the federal government, right?"

"Right."

"So any money we get will be replaced by Uncle Sam. Folks around here won't lose a red cent. And, if the government doesn't have enough cash, they can go to their friends at the Treasury and print more. No real harm done. Truly, Jade, it's the way of the West."

Jade turned and started walking back to Aunt Elise's, leaving Roy standing at that electrical box.

"Think about it," he called out after her. "That's all I'm asking!"

"Forget it," Jade called back.

"How can I forget that my parents need help? Tell me how to do that, Jade."

Jade didn't know what to say, so she just kept walking.

15

When she got back to her aunt's house, Jade switched on the small countertop fan and watched paper stars and Styrofoam planets dance across the ceiling. Those twists and turns eased her troubled heart. They lulled her into believing everything would be all right with the Parkers' store. They kept her from worrying about Roy's antics over at the Hammer and Nail or his warped idea to rob a bank.

"What are we going to do with that boy?" she asked Copernicus, who was stretched out in a triangle of sunlight by the refrigerator.

Copernicus rolled over, facing the opposite direction.

"You don't think I should encourage his idiotic plan, do you?"

Copernicus turned his head back and meowed.

"Well," Jade said, "then you're just as crazy. Two kids cannot rob a bank and get away with it."

Copernicus blinked.

"They can't!"

The cat licked his paws, stood up, and left the kitchen.

Jade leaned against the wall and closed her eyes. "I'm arguing with a cat," she said to the empty room. "A cat!"

"It happens to the best of us." Aunt Elise came through the back door. Tufts of dog fur dotted her sweater-vest. When she noticed Jade noticing, she said, "Astro likes to wrestle and Genghis Khan needs a cuddle from time to time, even if he won't admit it."

"They're lucky to have you."

She pulled pieces of straw from her sandals. "I was cleaning out one of the kennels. Mia went home today and both Sadie and Lady will go home tomorrow, but the Governor is coming, so that helps."

"The Governor?"

"I don't name them, I just love them. He's a black lab and full of get-up-and-go. I think you'll get along." She sat down at the table. "What were you arguing with Copernicus about?"

How could Jade even begin to explain? "Nothing, really."

"He's used to ruling the roost, so let me know if he needs a talking-to and I'll take care of it."

That made Jade smile.

"I'd typically microwave a frozen burrito for dinner, but I promised your mom I'd make more of an effort in the meal department. How about you help me put something together?"

Jade looked in the cupboards. They were filled with things like canned okra, canned tomatoes, canned tuna, canned spinach, canned pearl onions, canned Vienna sausages (which made Jade gag to even think about), canned chili, canned peaches, and canned kidney beans. "You got anything fresh?" she asked.

"All of those cans are fresh. I got them right before you came."

Jade tried the refrigerator. There was a plastic container that held the leftover stew, a few slabs of bacon, milk, cheese, and a dozen eggs. Those eggs gave her an idea.

"How about an omelet?" she said. "We can make it with bacon, onions, and cheese."

"Excellent!" Aunt Elise said, picking the dog fur off her sweater-vest and going over to the sink to wash her hands. "You take the lead."

Jade took the pearl onions from the cupboard, hoping a salt-and-butter sauté would help with their slimy, canned texture. "Where do you keep your nonstick pans?"

Aunt Elise pointed to the cast-iron skillet on the stove.

"That pan will sauté, fry, boil, and burn anything you want. It's multitalented."

Jade set to work: whisking and chopping and seasoning, making do with what they had. She lined bacon strips onto a plate and popped them in the microwave.

Aunt Elise grated the cheese. "Where did you learn to cook?"

"My mom taught me some things, but mostly I figured it out on my own. I'm not very good."

"I disagree, this smells delicious."

Jade kept stirring the onions, trying to keep them from burning in the pan. "It won't be perfect," she said.

"Who cares about that? Perfect has no personality."

Jade poured in the whisked eggs and sprinkled the cheese and microwaved bacon on top. She flipped the omelet over, pushing the broken middle back together and let it finish cooking.

"Now this is a meal with character," Aunt Elise said when Jade set the mound of egg and cheese in front of her. She took a bite. "Scrumptious!" She clicked her tongue twice and Copernicus came bounding in. "We've a chef in the house," she said to the cat, cutting a corner of the omelet and dropping it onto the floor. He sniffed, wary. "I didn't cook it, I swear." Copernicus glanced at Jade and started eating.

"Roy showed me around County Hardware today," Jade said, starting another omelet for herself.

Aunt Elise slowly twirled the fork in her hand and then gently placed it on her plate. "That empty store is a sad sight. Which reminds me." She went over to the counter and picked up a stack of flyers. "Voilà!"

They were exactly what Jade had hoped for. Stars lined the edges and a soft, curly font spelled out all the information. "I've also made a note of places you can take them to, like the YMCA and the Scout Council." She pulled out a list outlining nearly every business in Wellington. "You are an incredible young lady," Aunt Elise said, sitting back down and eating her shabby omelet like it was straight from Wolfgang Puck.

Jade flipped her eggs over in the pan. "I don't know if I'd call this food *incredible*."

"Wrong!" Aunt Elise shoved her fork in the air. "It is beyond that. But I wasn't talking about the food. I was most definitely talking about you and your brilliant idea to help the Parkers." Copernicus mewed for a second helping. "Traitor," Aunt Elise said, sliding another chunk of her omelet in front of the cat.

Jade looked up at the glittering stars and planets dangling above her head. She thought of Roy standing in front of Wells Fargo, staring at that electrical box and fighting so hard to find a solution for his family. "What if it's not enough?"

"It will all work out, you'll see."

"How can you be so certain?"

"I'm not certain," Aunt Elise said, fiddling with her fork again. "But I'm hopeful. And in tough situations like this, hope can go a long way."

16

Jade sat on Mr. Parker's red bar stool in their garage. She had told Aunt Elise she was going to spend the day exploring Wellington with Roy and went over early to try to talk him out of working for Farley. She found him elbow deep in the scattered parts of his dad's glassblowing kiln, determined to make it shine like new.

"Does your dad know you're fiddling with his oven thing?"

Roy let out a sigh. "It's a kiln, and I'm cleaning, not fiddling." He examined the end of a blackened pipe. "We can't ask top dollar if it's all grimy. And yes, he knows I'm out here."

"Has he agreed to sell it?"

"No, but I'm hoping he'll change his mind. It's a big

part of my plan to get our family back in business. That's what will make him happy."

"Are you sure about that?"

Roy stopped scrubbing. "Sure I'm sure."

"Well," Jade said, "we also have Aunt Elise's astronomy classes. I brought these flyers to take around town."

"That's good, but it's only one piece of the puzzle. We need a lot more money and we need it faster." He dipped the pipe into a bucket of soapy water and stifled a laugh. "I went by Farley's store this morning and there were trucks from two different cleaning companies out front. But I don't think they've found all the fish pieces because the place still looks pretty empty."

"Don't you feel bad about that?"

Roy frowned. "Don't forget who the real victims in this situation are. Losing a few days of business won't kill a guy like Farley. It may shake him up and have people in town look at his store differently, but we both know fish heads won't close his doors." He put the cleaned pipe down and picked up a different piece. "And what's wrong with having fun along the way? You have to admit it *was* funny to watch those people leave the store with their noses pinched shut."

Jade walked over to two large contraptions that looked

like brick and steel tubs, lying on their sides. "What's this stuff?"

"The smaller one is the furnace. It melts the glass rods and is where you do the gathering. And the bigger one is called the glory hole. It's where you maintain the heat of the glass to shape it." Roy walked over to a stack of long steel poles and picked one up. "Let me walk you through it."

"Is it safe?" Jade asked.

"Since the furnace isn't running it is. Everything is cold now. Once it gets going though, we can't be in here without my dad. The kiln gets to be about twenty-three hundred degrees Fahrenheit."

"I didn't know there was a twenty-three hundred degrees."

Roy walked over to the sideways tub and opened a small door. "The bowl inside this furnace is called a crucible. It holds the melted glass. You start by putting your blowpipe into the liquid glass and twisting a little bit onto the end of the pipe. It's kind of like cotton candy . . . the way you twist it onto the pipe one layer at a time."

He walked over to a workbench covered with tools that looked like huge salad tongs and wooden ladles. "Then you shape the glass with these, layering on more glass as you build your piece. Your final step is to put it in the kiln over here for the annealing process."

"What's that?" Jade said, struggling to keep it all straight.

"Annealing is when you allow the glass to cool slowly. That keeps it from cracking. Got it?"

"Got it." She ran her hand along the opening of the kiln. "It sure seems lousy to have to get rid of this stuff."

"I know." Roy set the wires down. "But once the store gets going again, my dad can replace it. There's always glass equipment for sale online, but the store lease only has until the end of summer."

Jade began to see how a boy like Joshua Parker could become Roy Parker. How his whole purpose was built around following his grand dreams . . . and how he expected that same level of devotion in others.

She had to ask. "I understand that you like Butch Cassidy and that you've learned all about him. But what are the real chances of you being related? I mean, Parker is a pretty common last name."

"Maybe," Roy said, "but Butch was raised in Beaver and Circleville, Utah. That's just a short ride from here." He picked up a dish towel and began drying the pipes. "It may be a common last name, but not all of those people are from the exact same area as the original Roy Parker. Besides, I feel a real connection to him. I don't need to prove anything to myself. I only want the paperwork to close the mouths of some kids at school."

"You use your nickname at school, too?"

"I use it everywhere," Roy said, defensive. "It's who I am."

Jade could guess Roy had a hard time with other kids. Cowboys were likely accepted, but not ones who claimed such royal descent. "What's stopping you from sending away for your genealogy today?"

He rubbed his finger and thumb together. *"Dinero."*

"How much will it cost?"

"Three hundred dollars for the complete set of records. I'm going to hire a specialist to track my line all the way back to the 1800s."

"Well," Jade said, "I hope you're able to do that real soon."

"Me, too. Which reminds me"—Roy looked at his watch—"we better get going. Farley's expecting us."

"Do you honestly think we should take that job? What if Farley's dangerous?"

Roy began piling the furnace pieces back into a cardboard box. "He's a slimeball without a conscience, but I'm not sure he's smart enough to be dangerous. Besides, I can handle myself and I need to get inside that ranch and see how Farley works. You're not going to go along with my bank-robbing plan, so this may be our only chance to find a way to bring him down."

"Regardless of the consequences?"

Roy shoved the box aside, left the workshop, and started walking. Jade grabbed the flyers and followed. She didn't want to. What she wanted to do was take Roy by the shoulders and shake him and tell him to knock it off. She wanted to remind him he was the one who said Farley was a snake and that they both needed to stay away.

But none of that would change Roy's mind. Kip Farley was offering a job, a shot at possible information, and, even more intriguing, a way for Roy to work on a real ranch.

It was more than the boy could resist.

17

Mucking out stalls was not Jade's idea of fun.

"A ranch hand has to start somewhere," Roy said when she complained.

Jade pointed to a man riding a chestnut mare in the field. He pulled on the reins, dancing the horse behind a cluster of goats. "That," she said, "is a ranch hand. What you are is a reeking stable boy." Her face was crumpled up from the stench of sweat and manure baking in the summer heat.

Roy looked right through Jade and out across the acres of grass and tidy rail fences that composed Kip Farley's property. Then he tucked his chin down and got back to work. "No one is forcing you to stay."

Jade stepped outside the stable. The air was heavy and

thick. She wiped her brow with the back of her hand, causing the beads of sweat to form a trickle down her cheek. The brilliant sun hung low and oppressive in the sky—not a single cloud in sight.

A bell clanged out across the stagnant heat.

"Lunchtime," Roy said, leaning his pitchfork against a post.

"Thank heavens, I'm starving."

"Right," Roy said, knocking Jade's shoulder with his as he passed, "all that bellyaching must have worked up quite an appetite."

"I helped."

"If pushing around hay and complaining at every turn is helping, then you sure did."

"What's your problem?"

"Look, I'm here to do a job. Either you're with me or you're not. Decide now because I'm tired of you bringing me down." He reached his hand out. "For once in your life, take a chance."

Jade bit her bottom lip. Slowly, she raised her arm and placed her hand over his.

Roy wrapped his fingers around hers and smiled. "Off we go," he said.

Lunch was taquitos, red rice, and pinto beans with squares of white onion floating in the sauce. All of it steaming hot. Anita, the root beer woman, served the food to a line of workers from behind a wide plank table. She was short and frail with apple-leather skin draping from her pointed cheekbones and scrawny arms.

"Back of the line," she snapped, smacking a heavily tattooed worker's hand with her bean ladle. He had tried to cut in front of Jade and Roy. Tiny as the woman was, her voice let everyone know who was in charge. "Plate," she said when Jade stepped up. Jade raised her plate. The woman plopped a ladle of beans and a spoonful of rice into the middle. "Two taquitos," she said. "No wasting." When Roy stepped up behind Jade, the woman did the same thing but gave Roy a once-over and said, "Three taquitos."

Roy stood up tall like he had been awarded the lunch grand prize. He loaded three fat taquitos onto his plate as the woman said "Five taquitos" to the man in line behind him. Roy ran his eyes over the hulking five-taquito man and dropped his shoulders. Jade held back a giggle.

"Let's sit over here." Roy started for an empty table in the blistering sun.

Jade eyed the crowded tables under the shade of three massive pines but Roy was already sitting down. She kicked her tennis shoe in the dirt and followed. "It's hot over here," she said once she got to the table.

"True," Roy said. "But this spot has the best view."

Jade looked at Farley's main house off to the right. "What's to see?"

"We can scope out *la casa*. Get the lay of the land," Roy said, shoving a taquito into his mouth.

"Is it necessary to talk like that?"

"Talk like what?" Roy swallowed and leaned over the table. "I saw him put his dog in the pickup and leave when we were stacking hay. I'm pretty sure the house is empty."

"Pretty sure?"

"Cowboy up, Jade. Farley's gone. His housekeeper is busy serving field hands." He shoveled down three scoops of beans, pushed his plate aside, stood up, and twisted his belt buckle. "This is our chance to take a quick peek inside."

Jade grabbed a taquito and followed Roy as he ducked to the side of a barn and around the back of the main house. He walked crouched over, shoulders hunched, as if that would somehow make him invisible. When he got to the back door, he knocked. "Just in case," he said.

When no one answered, he turned the brass knob, pushed the door open, and stepped into Kip Farley's mudroom. "You take left and I'll take right."

"Wait," Jade said. "What are we looking for?"

"Opportunities." He peeled off to the right and Jade went through the kitchen and down the hallway to the left, which led to the living room.

Oil paintings hung on every square inch of wall.

Every.

Square.

Inch.

They were side by side, top to bottom. Horses and mountains and lakes and buffalo—each frame crowding the next. Above the couch was a bright orange, red, and black painting of round, soft poppy petals.

Jade reached out and touched the bumpy golden frame.

"Psst!" Roy called from behind her. "No touching."

"I think this is an O'Keeffe."

"O-who?"

"Georgia O'Keeffe is a famous Western painter. We studied her in art last year."

Roy looked at the paintings covering the walls. "What a mess."

"Look at this one." She pointed to a painting of a purple-and-green buffalo head. "I can't remember who the artist is, but I know it's someone important."

"So this is what he did with the money he got from grinding our family business into the pavement?"

"Gallery-quality pieces like these don't come cheap."

"I told you he was a snake."

"It's not a crime to be successful," Jade said, walking over to a bronze sculpture of a bucking bronco on an end table.

"How much you figure something like that is worth?"

"Hard to say for sure, but I know it's a lot."

Roy's eyebrows jumped up. "For that?"

"Farley has good taste."

"Interesting," Roy said. "I've seen enough here. Let's scoot."

"Gladly."

Just then the back door opened with a clanging of pots and pans. Roy raised his finger to his lips and jerked his head toward the front door. Jade nodded. As the two slid out, she noticed a horseshoe nailed to the wall beside the door frame. It was turned with the ends pointing up to heaven. *That's for good luck,* Jade mouthed.

Roy flipped the horseshoe upside down and whispered, "It's about time your luck ran out, Kip Farley."

18

Apricot-tinted light dissolved into the red dirt of Aunt Elise's yard, making everything look soft and golden. Jade had worked all day at Farley's ranch and then walked across town with Roy, passing out the astronomy-class flyers. Her legs felt like noodles with tennis shoes at the ends.

Aunt Elise was leaning against a post at the corner of her front porch, scratching Astro behind the ears. His tongue dangled out the side of his mouth and his eyes were slit with pleasure. A large black dog sat up by the front door, tail thumping loudly against the planks.

"Long day?" Aunt Elise asked when Jade came up.

"Sure was." Jade motioned to the new dog. "Is this the Governor?"

Hearing his name sent his tail into overdrive. "The one and only," Aunt Elise said. "What were you two doing?"

"Roy took me to see some horses." It was mostly true.

Aunt Elise raised an eyebrow, gave Jade a curious look, and then went back to scratching Astro's ears. "Well, that does sound like Roy. If it has anything to do with being a cowboy, he's all over it like a chicken on a june bug."

Jade laughed. "He sure is."

Lobo came loping around from the kennels with Yaz and Genghis Khan bouncing behind. The three dogs nudged one another, fighting for Jade's attention. Emerson, the beagle, saw Jade, sat down, and howled into the copper sunset. It all felt very welcoming, as if they had missed her.

"So . . ." Aunt Elise drew the word out long and easy. "I followed a recipe today." She was acting casual, but Jade could see a twinkle in her expression. "Are you hungry?"

"Famished." Jade followed her aunt into the kitchen, which smelled of thyme, butter, and sage.

"I started digging through some boxes of old books this morning and came across this." Aunt Elise held a red-and-white-checkered cookbook up high. "Your mother gave it to me as a gift years ago." She opened the book by tugging on a ribbon marker and placed it in front of Jade. "Behold our dinner!"

"Beef Stew Extraordinaire," Jade read. She tried to sound

positive, but couldn't help thinking about Aunt Elise's last attempt at stew.

"I did exactly as it said with the exception of one teeny tiny substitution."

Jade froze.

"I have a friend on the other side of town who raises buffalo," Aunt Elise said. "It makes for good stew meat because it's so lean. Did you know buffalo is one of the leanest meats? Certainly the leanest of any red meat."

"Buffalo?" All Jade could think of was that beautiful purple-green buffalo-head painting in Kip Farley's living room. "Is that even legal?"

Aunt Elise chuckled. "Of course it is. Buffalo is to Wyoming what cheesesteak is to Philly."

Jade was having a hard time imagining that to be true. Everyone in the world knew about Philly cheesesteaks.

"It was quite a production, which is what I hate about cooking," Aunt Elise prattled on, stirring the stew with a ladle, "but I wanted to make you something special."

Jade noticed carrot shavings and potato peels spread across the countertop and spilled onto the floor. She looked over by the stove where a butcher knife sat on a wooden cutting board, pink blood soaking into the grain. "Did you cut the buffalo meat on a wooden board?" Jade thought everyone knew never to cut meat on wood. You have to use plastic because the wood is soft and porous and harbors E. coli, which can make you sick. That's Food Network 101.

Aunt Elise stilled her ladle above a bowl. One side of her mouth fell down and her eyes got all wide. "Did I do it wrong?"

"No," Jade said, biting back the words that wanted to come. She sat down at the fully set table and pulled a napkin across her lap. "No," she said again. "It probably doesn't matter that much."

"Good," Aunt Elise said, placing the bowls and sitting down across from her niece. Expectation filled every corner of the room.

Jade took a bite.

Tender meat that tasted like the best cut of top-round beef melted across Jade's tongue. The sage, butter, and thyme that had perfumed the room melded with a slice of potato and minced onion to form an incredible bite. "Wow!" Jade said, swallowing. "It's good."

Aunt Elise sat up and dipped her spoon into her stew. "Don't look so surprised."

"Were you teasing about the buffalo?" Jade was hopeful.

"Nope. That's top quality bison meat."

Jade thought of how she had been trying to read a chapter from *Robinson Crusoe* before bed each night and how Crusoe stayed alive by eating the goats he raised on his island. Eating buffalo wasn't that bad, was it? At least not as bad as eating goats.

"Let's do stars tonight," Aunt Elise said. "You and me. The view is going to be astounding."

Jade remembered how relentless the sun had been that day, how there hadn't been a single cloud in the sky, and she knew her aunt was right. It would be a perfect night for stars.

19

Sadie and Lady's mom came to pick them up after dinner, so Jade and her aunt removed the old straw, scrubbed out the feed bowls, and piled in some fresh straw for whoever the next tenants might be. The Governor was staying in Mia's old space, which Aunt Elise had prepared the day before.

Once they were finished with the dogs, Aunt Elise reached a hand out to Jade. "The sky awaits."

When they got up the ladder, Aunt Elise tilted the two plastic beach loungers all the way back, so they were completely flat. "Come," she said.

Jade stretched out and looked up. She couldn't imagine it being prettier than her first night in Wellington, but it was.

"Striking, isn't it?" Aunt Elise said.

Jade let her eyes adjust to the dimensions of the sky stretching out across the universe. It was turquoise blue in front with a lining of deep sable behind. White, yellow, and pink stars floated in a delicate display. "It goes on forever."

"On a clear night like this, you can see up to fifteen hundred stars and thirty-seven constellations. There is actually a total of eighty-eight constellations, but only a portion can be seen from where we are."

"Do you know them all?"

"Most," Aunt Elise said. "But you don't have to know much to look at the stars. Technology makes it so easy. There are a few Web sites that will show you precisely which constellations will be in your neighborhood each night. You type in your information and a custom map is created. There's even an iPad app for stargazers." She moved over, right next to Jade. "Let's see if you remember where Arcturus is."

Jade searched the sky for the simple ladle shape of the Big Dipper. Once she found it, she mentally followed the handle out and down to the tip. Then she reached a finger up. "Find the end of the Big Dipper's handle and arc to Arcturus," Jade said, moving her arm out toward the left to a shining gem of a star. "There it is!"

"I'm impressed you remembered," Aunt Elise said.

"Teach me something else," Jade said.

Aunt Elise pressed in closer. "Okay. Do you see how Arcturus has a slightly orange-yellow tint?"

"I guess so."

"This next one is a blue giant. It's called Spica and while it's not quite as bright as Arcturus, it's still a real beauty." She took Jade's hand. "Once you've found Arcturus, you simply spike straight down to the southwest until you see the blue-tinged star above the rooftops. Arc to Arcturus and spike down to Spica." She moved Jade's hand down and to the left. "See it?"

"It does look blue."

Aunt Elise settled into her own seat. "Most people think the night sky is black and white, but they're wrong. If you take the time to look, it's incredibly colorful."

Jade was having fun. "Another one," she requested.

"How about a sky story? Find Arcturus again. If you look to the right, there is a well-defined arc of stars in the shape of a crown. Do you see it?"

"Not really." Even knowing a few stars, it still looked like a jumble of lights to Jade.

Aunt Elise pressed her cheek against Jade's and took her hand once again. "Looking north. Can you see it right there?"

Jade thought she could.

"That is the Corona Borealis, also called the Northern Crown. Do you know its story?"

"No," Jade said, breathing in the smell of soil and straw that was her aunt.

"In Greek mythology, it represents the crown worn by Ariadne when she married Bacchus, the god of wine. To commemorate their union, Bacchus lifted the crown of stones from Ariadne's head and placed it in the heavens. He wanted everyone to know they were now a family." Elise got real quiet. "Bacchus understood."

"What do you mean?"

"Bacchus knew family was the most important thing. That's what the stars do. They keep us connected."

Jade kept her face to the night. The more she stared at that sky, the closer it grew until it seemed to fall all around her. There were no lights from the city—no buses whizzing by or police sirens screaming.

It was just the complete, uninterrupted stillness of night.

And all that quiet got her mind wandering. She thought about taking Roy's hand and agreeing to the dangerous task of spying on Kip Farley. She thought about Mr. Parker possibly selling off his kiln and annealer to give his family a second chance. She thought about Roy longing for his genealogy, and finally, she thought about Aunt Elise at her side, having spent the afternoon reading recipes and peeling vegetables.

"You see," Aunt Elise said out of the stillness, "people the whole world over are wishing upon these same stars. Think of a friend from Philadelphia and imagine her sharing this moment with you."

Jade fiddled with her thumbs in her lap. She turned to her aunt, but it was too dark to see much more than a vague shape at her side.

"Are you imagining?"

"I'm imagining," Jade said.

"Can I tell you a secret?"

Aunt Elise continued before Jade could answer. "Before you came to visit, I'd lie up here by myself and imagine you—all the way over in Philadelphia—looking at the Big Dipper or Cassiopeia at the exact minute I was looking at them and maybe, just maybe, thinking of me here in Wellington." She kept quiet for the longest time before adding, "Were you ever looking?"

"I don't even know what Cassiopeia is," Jade said.

"No, I guess you wouldn't." Jade could hear the hope fall in Aunt Elise's voice.

"But," Jade added, guilt suddenly pressing on her chest, "I'd look at the Big Dipper sometimes."

"Really?"

"Sure. And even though I didn't know about your stargazing, I guess there were a few times when I wondered who was out there and if anyone might be thinking of me."

"It was me! I was thinking of you."

"At that exact moment?"

Aunt Elise slid her hand across the beach lounger and draped her warm fingers across Jade's wrist. "At every moment."

After it was all over, Jade settled into her room for the night and picked up her copy of *Robinson Crusoe* from the bedside table. She was reading chapter sixteen, where Crusoe and Friday are making a boat to save a group of stranded mutineers, when Copernicus came in. He bounded onto her bed and found a comfortable spot. She put the book aside, reached down, and pulled the cat into the curve of her belly, running a hand across his silky fur, feeling the vibration of his purr through her skin. It soothed her mind and allowed her to find sleep.

20

The moon was still faint and low in the morning sky when Jade took her book and left the dog ranch.

Buffalo grass, soggy from the morning dew, slithered against Jade's legs as she pressed across a field, exploring the neighborhood a bit more. She stopped at a wide oak to run a hand across its rough bark. Two snail trails twisted up the side of the tree, intertwining. The snails were long gone, but their silver ribbons lingered behind. She tilted her head back and looked into the branches. Blue sky dappled and shone between olive-green leaves.

She found a dry spot at the base of the oak and opened her book. It was slow reading at times because it was written so long ago, but Jade was determined to finish it. Both her mother and Aunt Elise loved the story and Jade had to admit that while she didn't like everything Crusoe did,

she was impressed with all he accomplished on that island.

"Out so early?"

Jade turned to see Tilly and Angelo by the road. Tilly
was pushing him along in his wheelchair.

"I was just exploring," Jade said, standing.

Tilly nodded. "Wyoming is good for that sort of thing."

Jade went over to the roadside.

"Care to join us on our walk?" Tilly asked. "I try to
take Angelo out every morning. The cool early air is good
for his lungs."

Angelo leaned over to Jade. "When I could walk at her
side, she would say that *we* liked to go for a stroll but now
that I'm in this awful chair she says Angelo needs this and
Angelo needs that. Like I'm three years old!"

"Don't let him scare you," Tilly said, pushing his wheelchair forward. "He may come off as gruff, but he's an old
softy on the inside."

"You're doing it again," Angelo said, but this time Jade
thought she saw a twitch of a grin hiding behind his shaggy
white mustache.

Jade walked with them. They talked about Angelo's years
working as a miner over in Campbell County, which she
learned was on the opposite side of Wyoming.

"Wyoming has a split personality," Tilly rambled on.

"Half is what you see here with these gorgeous landscapes and mountains, but the other half is unadorned, stark coal-mining fields. When the mines were finished with us, it was an easy decision to pick up and move over here to Wellington."

"It sure is different," Angelo agreed.

Tilly pushed Angelo's chair into their driveway and up the new ramp. He stood and ambled a few steps over to his rocker on the porch.

"I'll get us some orange juice," Tilly said, placing a blanket across Angelo's lap. "You two visit."

Angelo grumbled and looked over to Jade, who was hanging back in the driveway. "You heard the orders," he said, tilting his head to a bench at his side. "You've been put on babysitting duty."

Jade went over and sat down. "I'm sure that's not what she meant."

"Oh, it is," Angelo said. "But I know it's done out of love so I let it be."

Jade shuffled her tennis shoes along the planks of the porch and picked at imaginary lint on her jeans.

Angelo cleared his throat and asked, "How long have you been in Wellington now?" Jade noticed his tone was softer than usual.

"Six days."

"Are you having fun?"

"So far."

Angelo nodded. "Good. It's too bad you missed the Fourth of July. We celebrate that big out here. But there's the Juniper Festival coming up at the end of the month. Will you be around that long?"

Jade looked over to the screen door, wondering when Tilly would be coming back with the orange juice. "I'm going home on July twenty-ninth. That's a Monday."

"Great," Angelo said, swaying his rocking chair back and forth and running one hand down through his beard. "Then you won't miss it. And in the meantime, Elise tells us that Roy has been keeping you busy." He let out a gravelly laugh that turned into a cough. When his breath came back, he wiped his hand across his mouth and continued, "I don't suppose they have cowboys like Roy where you come from."

"Not many."

Angelo smiled. "Roy Parker is a true original." Then he noticed Jade's book. "That's an ambitious read for a young girl."

"I can manage," Jade said.

"I don't doubt that for a minute. What's your favorite part so far?"

Jade thought. "I'd say it was when Crusoe came across

the footprint in the sand after all that time thinking he was alone. That was a surprise."

Angelo pulled at the tips of his beard and nodded.

"But," Jade said, "I don't like how he made Friday into his slave once he found him. I wish they could have been friends."

"Hmph," Angelo said deep in his throat.

"My mom gave it to me to read. I guess it's kind of an obscure book."

"Obscure?" Angelo swayed his rocking chair forward.

"That means not very well known," Jade explained.

"That's not true."

"It was one of my spelling words last year," Jade said. "I'm pretty sure that's the definition."

Angelo let out another scratchy laugh. "Not the definition," he said. "I was referring to the *obscure* part. *Robinson Crusoe* has influenced more of our modern culture than you know."

Jade turned the book over in her hands. "Really?"

"Sure," Angelo said, going back to a steady rocking of his chair. "It was the first novel written about being stranded somewhere. There's a whole group of stories and movies based on it. Think of movies like *Life of Pi* or *Cast Away* or *The Island of Dr. Moreau*. Think of television shows like *Survivor* or *Lost* or even *Gilligan's Island*."

"Wow," Jade said.

"People call those kinds of shows robinsonade because their basic concept comes from that book you have right there. Have you ever played the game *Let's say you're stranded on a desert island . . . ?*"

"*What three people or books or things would you want with you?*" Jade asked.

"Yep." Angelo grinned. "It all comes from Crusoe."

"How do you know that?"

"You'd be amazed how many books I've read since being relegated to this chair." Angelo gave a pat to the worn arm of his rocker. "And believe me when I say that that *obscure* book you're reading summarizes what everyone wants in life."

Just then, the screen door squeaked open and Tilly came out carrying a tray of orange juice. "I took the liberty of calling Elise and letting her know you came by for a visit." She carried the tray to the opposite side of the porch and began pouring the juice into glasses.

Jade leaned in to Angelo, curious. "What does everyone want?"

"Adventure, of course." The words had barely fallen out when he crouched over and heaved in a jerky breath. His face turned as pink as the crocheted blanket Tilly had draped across his lap. Coughs tumbled out one after another. Tilly ran to his side and began slapping him firmly on the back, right between his broad shoulders. "Fine," he gasped between coughs. "I'm fine."

"Don't go scaring me like that, old man," Tilly said, worry twisted up on her brow.

Angelo's breath steadied. "Who are you calling an old man, old woman?"

Tilly shook her head. "Incorrigible."

And just like that, Angelo was back to grinning and rocking and lacing his leathered fingers through his beard.

21

Only a week after Jade pinned those flyers across Wellington, her aunt came dancing into her bedroom. "Morning Glory," Aunt Elise sang out as she pulled the maroon-checkered curtains open. "We have big work to do. Big work!"

Jade squinted against the bright sun and looked at the clock on her bed stand: 9:07.

Roy would be expecting her at Farley's. They had been mucking out stalls every day this past week. After their first day, Roy had gone to Farley's earlier and earlier, saying he was infiltrating Farley's world and helping his family in the process. Jade had a hard time understanding how shoveling manure in the scorching summer heat would help Mr. Parker reopen County Hardware. Still, she forced herself to join Roy whenever she could, but never before ten. It was summer vacation, after all.

Aunt Elise stood over the bed. "Guess what kind of phone call I got this morning?"

Jade mumbled something incoherent.

"It was a mother looking to book her daughter's birthday party on my roof." Aunt Elise couldn't contain herself. "For this Friday night! Can you believe it? There will be five girls, all ten years old, plus the mother. I'll teach and you'll bake. I hope you don't mind but I offered up your services to bake a cake."

"I've never made a birthday cake before."

"There has to be a first time for everything and I know you can do it."

Jade pressed her fist to her eyes and yawned. "Okay. How much did you charge for the cake service?"

Aunt Elise tilted her head to the side. "Here's the thing."

The moment those words came out, Jade knew it was bad.

"She was so excited about booking the party but said she only had enough money for her and her daughter. Isn't that terrible? Her tenth birthday and she wouldn't have a single friend attend. Anyway," Aunt Elise prattled on, folding the covers back and helping Jade sit up, "I told her to invite as many as four additional guests and not to worry about the money. That's when I had the idea to have you bake the cake. Isn't that wonderful?"

"But the whole point was to earn money for the Parkers. Six people would have made nearly a hundred dollars, plus you could have easily charged another thirty or so for the food. Why would you tell her not to pay you?"

"You're right. I should have thought it out more. But one event on my roof isn't going to make or break County Hardware." Her aunt was radiating joy. "I'm going to be an astronomy teacher. Me—a teacher!"

Jade flopped back on her bed. "Even a teacher gets paid."

"I honestly thought you'd be excited about this." The words were like delicate pieces of glass floating in the air.

Jade sat back up and put on a smile. "If they tell their friends, it could bring us more customers. Maybe it will be good advertising."

Aunt Elise raised her hand. "And I swear to be more business savvy from now on."

Jade wanted to believe her aunt, but doubt laced itself around that promise. "You'll be great," she said.

"We!" Aunt Elise twirled around the room in a dance. "We will be great together."

They ate a breakfast of cold cereal and then Aunt Elise pushed a piece of paper across the table toward Jade. "I've got some important errands to take care of this morning," she said. "Here are a few things you can help out with. Once the list is done, the day is yours."

"I'm supposed to hang out with Roy. Or maybe I could come with you." Jade was thinking how nice it would be to have an excuse not to join Roy over at Farley's ranch. "We can get the stuff for the birthday cake on our way home."

Aunt Elise stood up. "You'd be bored to tears if you came with me. I'll be at the dentist's office with the awful, oppressive smell of plastic and mouthwash and those painfully bright fluorescent lights. No, you take care of feeding the dogs and poop-scooping the kennels."

"Which is way more fun."

"Agreed." Aunt Elise grabbed her braided-rope satchel and headed out the back door.

Jade followed and watched from the doorway as Aunt Elise revved the old Lincoln and headed down the driveway in front of a yapping cluster of dogs.

When the gate was shut behind the car, the dogs turned back to Jade. Astro led the pack, coming up and nudging his head under her elbow for a pet. She ran her fingers along the base of his ears. Short brown fur shed onto her hands in clumps. "You need another good brushing in all this heat," she said.

Astro licked his teeth noisily and sat down with a *har-rumph*. His oversize tongue hung out of his mouth and strings of drool dangled from his chin.

"And a bib," Jade added.

Astro shook his head, flinging those thick cords of drool through the air and onto her nightshirt.

"Gross," Jade said, stepping back.

Astro raised his chin and pulled the sides of his mouth back into a satisfied smile.

"You think that's funny?"

Astro lowered his head and smacked a massive paw to the ground. Then he looked up and did that smile thing again.

Jade slowly sidestepped over to the corner of the house. "You're hilarious," she teased, spinning around to grab the garden hose. She turned the nozzle on, sending a stream of water barreling through the morning air, landing right at Astro's feet.

The dog jumped and danced and, as the blazing sky was her witness, laughed—jaw hanging open, tail wheeling and spinning through the air—unmistakable laughter.

Jade laughed, too. Deep and soulful, toes to fingertips. She whirled the garden hose in waves and spun it in spirals and danced right alongside Astro and the other dogs, who had joined in the water play. She snickered and chortled and hooted and giggled and, finally, she fell down on a small patch of grass lining Aunt Elise's front walk, exhausted.

Astro stood over her, panting. His breath was steamy and spiked with the saltiness of cheap kibble. Then he lay down, like a mountain, gently rolling into her side, and nudged his head up against her shoulder.

The other dogs lapped at the puddles and stretched out in the sunshine.

Jade kept her eyes closed and her smile wide.

Wyoming had turned out to be everything her aunt had promised.

22

Jade decided to take a roundabout way to meet Roy at Farley's ranch. She stopped by the YMCA to see if they needed more of her aunt's stargazing-course flyers. Standing there in front of the community bulletin board, surrounded by squawking children and the loud *thumps* of a basketball in the gymnasium, she found the perfect solution to County Hardware's problem:

WELLINGTON'S JUNIPER FESTIVAL
JULY 27
COWBOY POETRY CONTEST
GRAND PRIZE: $2,500

"You dropping off more of those flyers?" Sandy, the

YMCA receptionist, was reaching her hand out. "They go like hotcakes. Have you had any calls?"

"We have our first booking," Jade said.

"Doesn't surprise me a bit. Elise Bennett knows a thing or two about stargazing. I've been doing my best to talk it up as folks come through. Maybe I should come by and get a firsthand peek at what you ladies are doing over there."

Jade was still mesmerized by the announcement hanging in front of her. "What?" she said. "Oh, sure. You should come by." She tapped a finger on the flyer. "Is this for anyone?"

Sandy came over from behind the counter. "Sure is," she said. "We take our cowboy poetry seriously around here but I suppose anyone is welcome to enter."

"And they pay someone twenty-five hundred dollars for writing a poem?"

"Oh no," Sandy said. "Not any poem. It has to capture what we love about living out here in the West. I'm telling you, it's a real show."

Jade's heart started skipping. "Does it have to be one person, or can two work together?"

Sandy peered at the crinkled paper pinned to the corkboard. "Doesn't say. I imagine they'd allow a double entry. Why?"

"I have an idea for the perfect duo." Jade noticed there

were multiple flyers on the same pin. "Can I take one of these?"

"Knock yourself out," Sandy said, going back behind the counter. "But you don't have much time. The twenty-seventh is the end of next week."

Jade crammed a flyer into her pocket, thanked Sandy, and took off to find Roy.

When she got to Farley's barn it was just after two o'clock and she noticed how the hay was stacked in perfect rows off to the side, the main aisles were swept clean, and the stable doors were scrubbed, shining like new. "You've been busy today."

"I had given up on you," Roy said.

"Aunt Elise gave me a long list of chores and then I went by the YMCA."

"That's okay," Roy said. "Guess what? Farley said if I keep up the good work he'll let me move out of the stables and into the fields."

"To ride and wrangle?" Jade asked with a grin.

"I don't like working for a guy like Farley." Roy looked earnest. "But if I'm gonna be here checking things out, I might as well make the best of my time."

Jade wondered who he was trying to convince.

Roy walked to the window overlooking the main horse

141

pasture. The expression on his face said it all. He was dying to sit high in a saddle. Aching to feel the wind on his face and the reins in his hands.

"Have you ever been on a real horse, Roy?"

"When I was four I got to ride one of those ponies that go 'round and 'round in a circle at the state fair. You know, the ones that are too fat and old so they tie them into that contraption and sell rides for two dollars." He hung his head. "I suppose it doesn't count for much, but I'll never forget that day."

"How can that be? This is Wyoming. Horses are every-where. Even the license plates have a picture of that buck-ing bronco on them. How could you, of all people, go all these years and never get a chance to ride?"

"If you haven't noticed, my parents aren't exactly the riding type."

Jade took the paper from her pocket and held it out. "Look at what I found on the YMCA's bulletin board."

"The Juniper Festival," he said. "We go every year."

"More than the festival. *This.*" She pointed to the section about the cowboy poetry. "Twenty-five hundred dollars goes to the winner. That's a whole summer of shoveling manure over here."

"Are you feeling poetic?"

"Your mom is a poet, Roy!"

"My mom writes about political stuff like America's indifference to third-world countries. This"—he shook the paper—"has to be about cowboy life."

"That's the beauty of it! You know everything there is to know about being a cowboy. You can help her write the winning poem."

Gears started to turn in Roy's head—Jade could see it. "Maybe," he said.

"And the best part is you won't have to work here anymore. You'll have your summer back."

"Why wouldn't I work here? We need every dime we can get our hands on. I like this festival idea, but that doesn't mean I can quit. It may look like I'm playing around over here, but I'm not." He jumped away from the window and grabbed a pitchfork. "Farley's comin'." He began fluffing hay. "And I've got a whopper planned for him today. Some good ole cowboy magic is about to go down."

Jade started to ask Roy what he was up to, but Farley strolled through the stable doors and stopped her questions. "It looks right smart in here," Farley said in his polished way. "It's been a full week, so I've come with your pay."

Roy set aside his pitchfork and grabbed a clipboard from atop an overturned wooden box. "I've been grateful for the opportunity to work, sir. And I was hoping I could appeal to your charitable side today and ask you about a possible donation for Wellington's Boys and Girls Club." He stood up tall, wiped sweaty strands of hair back from his face, and held the clipboard out toward Farley. "They're running a big campaign right now."

Farley took the clipboard and eyed it. "Is that right?"

Roy tried to stand up taller. "Any amount would be appreciated. A smart businessman like yourself could make a difference in our community. That's the pledge card right there." Roy gestured to the clipboard.

"I suppose I could make a donation," Farley said.

Roy whipped out a pen from his back pocket and handed it to Farley, who filled in his name, address, and a signature pledge of fifty dollars on the card.

"Thank you very much," Roy said, taking back the pen and clipboard. "I knew we could count on you."

Farley nodded and pulled a folded wad of cash from his front pocket. He peeled off two one-hundred-dollar bills and held them out to Roy. "Now back to our business here on the ranch. Quality pay for quality work."

Roy stared at the money, like the reality of that cold hard cash waving in front of him was too much to hope for. "Thank you," he said, finally taking the money.

Then Farley turned to Jade. "Your hours have been a little less. I'd say one-fifty should make us even."

Jade took the crisp bills.

Farley grinned and played with the ring of keys on his belt loop. "It's a good job you've done here. Why don't you knock off early today?" He walked over and took the pitchfork from Roy's hands. "My puncher, Stuart, will be expecting you tomorrow morning at seven sharp. You'll be working with him from now on and he doesn't like to be kept waiting."

"Puncher?" Jade asked.

Roy was grinning wide as the canyons around them. "That's a hired hand who works on horseback." He turned to Farley. "No sir, I surely won't keep him waiting."

Farley turned to Jade. "You're welcome to ride as well, if you're interested."

Jade saw this as an opportunity to excuse herself from continuing to work for Farley. "Thanks for the offer, but I could never make it by seven. My aunt needs help with the dogs in the mornings. Besides, ranch work hasn't been my favorite, so I think I'll turn in my resignation."

"Suit yourself," Farley said, giving a nod and heading back into the fields.

"Here." Jade held out her pay toward Roy. "Add this to the County Hardware fund. Three hundred and fifty dollars is a good start."

Roy blinked slowly. He took the money and put it into his back pocket. "Thanks."

"Congratulations on working with Farley's puncher. It's what you wanted, right?"

"Yeah," Roy said, bringing back his grin. "I suppose it is."

"Are you upset I won't be working over here anymore or coming to ride with you?"

"Nah, a city girl like you would only slow me down."

Jade knew he was teasing. "We've got the rest of the afternoon," she said. "What do you want to do?"

Roy leaned back and looked out the door, making sure no one was there. Then he stepped over to Jade's side and whispered, "Reconnaissance."

23

Butch spent many an afternoon crouched in bushes just like these." Roy pushed a stray branch from the box elder bush out of his face. They were hiding in the empty field across from Farley's front gate. "His line of work was ninety-five percent patience."

"What was the other five percent?"

"Taking people by surprise. You have to wait for the perfect moment before moving in, a moment when you are at your highest point of awareness and the other guy is at his lowest. Anything short of that will land you in jail."

"Did Butch ever land in jail?"

"He spent eighteen months in a Wyoming cell but he told Governor Richards that if he was released he'd never commit another crime in Wyoming."

"And did he keep that promise?"

Roy gave Jade a wounded look. "Of course he kept it."

Jade twisted around, trying to find a spot where branches weren't jabbing her in the ribs. "And what's your plan for taking Farley by surprise? What's that cowboy magic you were talking about back in the barn?"

Roy was smug. "You were there, didn't you see? I convinced him to make a huge donation to the Boys and Girls Club."

"Fifty bucks?" Jade asked flatly.

"Well, it started out that way, but Farley was stupid enough to use the pen I offered him so I'm going to be able to go back in and add a few zeros to that pledge card."

"How many zeros?"

"Two sounds about right," Roy said.

"You think Farley's going to pay five thousand dollars? He'll say you rigged the numbers and you'll get in all sorts of trouble."

"Highly unlikely given the second half of my plan." Roy seemed so pleased with himself. "When it comes time to collect the donation, I'll put a call in to every media source we have here in town. Newspaper? Check. City Hall? Check. Ron's local cable channel? Absolutely. Then I'm going to go get a big ole bundle of helium balloons from Albertson's Market, gather a bunch of kids from the club, and we're all going to meet up at Farley's store. Sure, he can say he only pledged a pathetic fifty bucks but I'm banking on the fact he'll be too embarrassed to admit his cheapskate ways. See how he'll be taken by surprise in that moment? If half the town is there to celebrate his incredibly generous donation of five grand to the needy youth of our community and the only way he can save face is to write a fat check? Trust me, he'll pony up the cash. The Boys and Girls Club will get a solid donation and we get to see Farley squirm."

Jade shook her head. "It's brilliant, but it's wrong."

Roy thumped his clipboard. "It's what I call pullin' a Butch Cassidy."

"You'll get fired, though. You know that."

"Yeah," Roy said, "but the campaign isn't over for a few more weeks. A few weeks of riding with Farley's puncher and collecting pay is good enough for me."

The front gate to Farley's began to crank open. Roy pulled Jade even lower into the bushes as Farley's white pickup truck eased onto the road, his black rottweiler hanging its head out the window.

"Finally," Jade said, standing up. "My legs are killing me."

Roy pulled her back down. "We've got another fifteen minutes." He looked at his watch. "His housekeeper doesn't leave until five-thirty."

"But what if Farley comes back?"

"Then it'll have to wait for another day."

The thought of sitting like a flattened pretzel in the searing sun for another afternoon nearly made her cry. "I don't see why we have to be in these bushes. No one can see us on this side of the gate."

Alarm passed over Roy's eyes. "The whole town of Wellington can see us. Anyone driving by or taking their dog on a walk can see us. One kid coming home from the market and our cover would be blown to smithereens."

Jade sat back down. The summer sun was in no hurry to set, and beat down on them with a vengeance. Finally, when the longest fifteen minutes of Jade's life had passed, Farley's housekeeper, Anita, left on a worn-out motor scooter.

Roy didn't say a word. Each lift of eyebrow or twist of lip told Jade when to walk and when to lag behind another bush. They moved in jerks and jolts from one bush to another until they were at Farley's back door.

"What makes you think it will be unlocked?" Jade whispered.

Roy twisted the doorknob, pushing the door open. "I told you," he whispered back. "People are entirely too trusting. Now not another word." He crooked a finger, inviting her to follow him into the mudroom. They sat on the floor quietly for a moment, listening for the possibility of people in the house. When Roy was sure it was empty, he stood up and moved with more ease.

Jade followed him through the kitchen, down the hallway, into the dining room. The silence in the house was oppressive and she found herself looking along the ceiling for traces of cameras or alarm boxes. She started to tell Roy they should leave, but his lips were pressed firmly together—a warning not to speak. The quiet was so thick, she almost felt like speaking would break a spell and send alarm bells screaming in the air.

Roy came to an abrupt stop, causing her to bump into his back. "All right," he whispered. "Let's start taking inventory."

"Of what?"

Roy pulled out his pen, followed by a blank piece of paper from the back of the clipboard, and handed them to Jade. "I want a list of pieces you think might bring a price and the name of the artist if it's marked on the piece. I'll be taking pictures."

"What for?"

"I've done enough for others by donating Farley's money to the Boys and Girls Club. Now it's time to take a piece for County Hardware."

"I'm not stealing anything." Jade shoved the pen and paper back into Roy's hands.

"Man, you really are a lousy sidekick. First, you wimp out on my bank-robbing plan and now you're bellyaching about making a simple list. I'm not asking you to steal anything. I'll be the one to post this junk on eBay and when the orders come in, I'll find a way to get the pieces out of here. The only thing you have to do is write down some information and help me figure out what this stuff is worth. Why did you sneak in here if you weren't willing to help?"

"You're better than this, Roy. I get the whole Boys and Girls Club—donation trick and the fish heads and alarm clocks going off down at the Hammer and Nail, but setting up an eBay account to sell stolen goods is illegal."

"Ease up, that's what half of eBay is!"

"No it's not."

"Fine," Roy said. "Just stay out of my way." He started with the bronze bucking-bronco statue on the living room side table. He picked it up and peeked underneath, then pulled out his phone and began taking pictures.

"Farley will notice when stuff starts to go missing," Jade pressed.

"I'm not gonna sell his big pieces. Just a few of the small ones he won't miss right away. Shhh!" He raised a hand.

The crunch of tires over gravel moved along the side of the house.

Roy snapped another picture, this one of a blue fluted dish on a bookshelf, then jerked his head sideways and they snuck out the front door as Farley came in through the back.

24

When Jade knew Roy was busy with Farley's puncher the following morning, she went to see Mr. and Mrs. Parker. "It's because I care about him," she said, sitting on their green-flowered couch and feeling like the biggest snitch in the world.

"Of course you do, dear." Mrs. Parker was sitting across from Jade and leaning in, elbows on knees.

"And I'm worried he might be too close to trouble."

"Oh my," Mrs. Parker said, head bobbing. "Then it's good you came to me."

Jade looked around the room. "Where's Mr. Parker?"

"William is hanging a door for a neighbor."

"Oh." Jade plucked at yellowed stuffing poking out of a small rip in the couch.

"But you go ahead and tell me what's on your mind. If Roy is in some kind of trouble, we need to know."

Jade tried to ignore the snitch feeling growing inside her chest, right below her rib cage, over where her heart usually sat.

Mrs. Parker reached forward and took Jade's hand. "I promise not to tell Roy you came, if that helps at all."

It did. Somehow those words gave Jade the final push she needed. "Roy took a job working for Kip Farley. We both did actually, but I've quit going. He's cleaning out the stables and Farley promised to teach him how to ride." The words were rushing along like a steam loco-motive on a one-way track to tattle town. "He has this crazy idea about earning enough money to reopen your store and he's going overboard to make it happen." When she was finished there wasn't a speck of air in her lungs.

Mrs. Parker leaned back in her chair and smiled. "Is that what this is about? We've known he's been working for Kip Farley all along. Why else would I let him dis-appear for hours at a time with flimsy explanations like 'They're giving two-for-one ice cream cones at the Dairy Quip'? It doesn't take all day to get ice cream and you certainly don't come home from it sweaty and smelling like manure. Mr. Farley called and asked our permission back when he hired you two."

"So Aunt Elise knows, too?"

"She does."

"Why haven't you guys said anything about it?"

Mrs. Parker moved over to the couch and began picking at the same tuft of stuffing. "Being a parent is a juggling act and sometimes we have to be creative. If Roy knew we were aware of his work at Farley's, he might not enjoy it as much, so we asked Elise to play along and allow him this experience by not saying anything to you. I think he's keeping it hush-hush because he doesn't want to hurt our feelings, given the situation with William's store, but I'm happy he's found a place over there. Working on a real ranch must be so much fun for him. You know, it's not Kip Farley's fault our store closed down. Things like that happen to small businesses all the time."

"That's not what Roy thinks."

"Roy is a twelve-year-old boy who lets his imagination run wild at times. He'll figure things out on his own soon enough. And, the truth is, William was far better at dealing with customers than he was running the actual business. Roy may have a hard time seeing it, but closing the store was a relief for his dad."

"Have you told Roy that?"

"We've tried." She let out a soft laugh. "But Roy hears what Roy wants to hear."

Jade knew that was true. "The problem is"—this was where Jade chose her words with care—"I'm worried he might be doing things over at Farley's that he shouldn't."

"Like what?" Mrs. Parker asked.

Jade sighed. She was willing to tell enough to let Roy's parents know they should check in on him, but she wasn't willing to rat him out completely. "I just think you should talk to him."

"Okay," Mrs. Parker said. "I'll talk to him."

Jade reached into her pocket and pulled out the Juniper Festival flyer. "I got this over at the YMCA. It's a poetry contest and I thought you could enter."

Mrs. Parker took the paper. "I do love a good poetry reading, but I'm afraid I'd fail miserably at this one. I have lived most of my adult life in Wyoming, but I know shamefully little about classic Western life."

"That's the beauty of it," Jade said. "You know poetry and Roy knows everything about being a cowboy. He could tell you the facts and you could transform them."

"My writing has to come from deep within my heart. It has to be a subject matter I feel strongly about."

"Roy feels strongly about campfires and cattle hauls. It could also be about simple things like the weather or the prairie."

"It would be nice to work together. Was he interested?"

"I think so."

Mrs. Parker read the flyer again. "I guess our first order of business is convincing him." She took the flyer into the kitchen and stuck it behind a Scrabble-letter magnet on the refrigerator. "Let me plead our case. I'll strike up a fire in the pit out back and have a weenie roast where we cook hot dogs on skewers and eat pork and beans right out of the can." She turned to Jade. "It softens him up every time."

25

On Friday, as Jade walked home from Farley's, cool wind teased the sweetness from the trees. It was Roy's second day riding with Stuart and Jade had gone by to watch him—sitting high on his black mare and wearing a smile that could stretch all the way back to Philly. Stuart taught him how to dance the horse behind the goats and guide them from one field into another. Roy never had to be told how to do something twice.

Jade pulled out her phone and looked at the time. Five ten-year-olds would be coming for Aunt Elise's first stargazing course in a little while and she had to finish frosting the cake. She picked up her pace. Sagebrush dotted out across the fields like silver freckles on a beige landscape. Gauzy clouds layered the sky above in varying shades of pink. And as always, the Tetons stood watch over their valley. Jade looked up at those raspberry-swirled clouds and thought about Tilly in her pink house—how she would love the sky at that moment.

Aunt Elise was sitting on the step of her front porch, sleeping dogs huddled around her, when Jade came up the driveway. "How is Roy's riding coming along?"

"He's a natural," Jade said. "I still can't believe you knew we were working for Farley."

"There's no harm in a little covert adventure. That's the kind of stuff Roy lives for." Then she looked down to the dogs and gave Lobo a pat on the head. "Let him have his secret for now. He seems to be having such fun."

The memory of Roy taking inventory in Farley's living room came creeping back and Jade wondered if she was making the right decision by keeping that information to herself.

"I had to cancel the party tonight," Aunt Elise said.

"Why?"

"Storm's blowing in, and it looks like a doozy."

Jade turned back to the raspberry sky. Far behind the swirls were heavy, soot-colored clouds. "Are you sure those aren't the kind of clouds that make a lot of noise but don't do much else? What if we passed out umbrellas?"

"Nope," Aunt Elise said. "It wouldn't be safe to allow the party to go on. I remember this particular rule from my Intro to Business class back in college: Allowing children to get sizzled by lightning will quite often hurt your bottom line.

"The good news is, we got a booking for a Boy Scout merit-badge class for Monday and the weather report looks more hopeful."

"Will the birthday party reschedule?"

"No," Aunt Elise said. "Her mom said they'd make other plans. She really wanted to celebrate her daughter's birthday on the actual day."

"But what about the cake? I spent all morning on it, not to mention the fresh-squeezed lemonade and strawberry tea in the refrigerator."

"It'd be a shame to have it go to waste," Aunt Elise agreed. "Hey!" She slapped her hands on the step, which sent Lobo and Yaz skittering away. "How about I invite the Parkers over? We can batten down the hatches and have an old-fashioned storm watch."

"What's that?"

"You know, we turn off all the lights, sit by the windows, and eat goodies while counting lightning strikes." She pushed Emerson off her lap. "I'll give them a quick call. And it'd probably be a good idea to tarp the kennels for the dogs, too."

"Should we bring them in?"

"Copernicus would have a heart attack. They all have good houses and warm, dry straw to climb into. If we cover the chain link on their kennels to keep the heavy winds and rain out, they'll be fine."

Jade looked up at the sky again. Already, the delicate pink clouds were fading against a backdrop of darkness. Red dust, whipped up by a sudden wind, whirled in the air, making the whole place look like a faded picture in a Western storybook. One raindrop fell on Jade's shoulder, and another on her cheek. "I'll never understand the weather out here."

"It's like we say: Welcome to Wyoming. If you don't like the weather, just wait five minutes. Let's get the pups safe."

Jade began herding the dogs into their respective homes. First the Governor, followed by Lobo, Yaz, Emerson, Jack, and Astro. "You, too," Jade said to Genghis Khan, who was stretched out on a grassy spot on the lawn. "Come on." He clearly had no intention of moving.

Astro snorted and grumbled at him. Genghis Khan must have known size wins out over stubborn every time because he slowly stood up and moseyed over to his pen. "Thanks for your help," Jade said, reaching her fingers through the chain link of Astro's kennel and rubbing them across his nose.

Aunt Elise came around from the garage, pulling a stack

of plastic tarps behind her. "They're coming," she said, referring to the Parkers. "And they're in the mood for cake, too."

"Great." Jade was glad her morning of preparation hadn't been wasted.

A small dirt devil twisted and skipped across the yard, snatching up dead leaves and clumps of dog fur as it went. "We need to tie these tarps across the roof of each kennel, as well as on the north and west sides—that's the path this tempest is on," Aunt Elise said. The wild-rose bushes bent and swayed under the pressure of the wind and purple petals flitted off into the hazy sky.

Jade helped her aunt drape and lash the heavy tarps to the posts of each kennel, blocking out the wind and offering each dog a snug area to relax in. She turned their plywood houses to face east and pushed clean straw around each arched doorway. As she worked, the wind kept getting stronger and the raindrops kept landing closer and closer together.

Aunt Elise double knotted the last rope to the last fence post. "Good work," she said, wiping her forearm across her brow. "Feel that heat? There's about to be a huge crash between this hot air lingering above us and a cold front moving in from Canada. Conditions like these make for dangerous storms."

Once inside, Aunt Elise piled candles and matches and two LED lanterns onto the kitchen table. "The Parkers said they would bring a game," she said.

"Which one?"

"Clue, I think."

Solving a murder in the midst of a pounding storm sounded creepily fun.

"I hope I get to be Miss Scarlet," Aunt Elise said. "I love Miss Scarlet. How's the storm coming?"

Jade looked out the kitchen window. The clouds in the distance were much closer. Their undersides were shredded and reaching down to the earth . . . smudged like a chalk picture. Aunt Elise came up beside her. "See how they pull down to the ground like that?"

"Yeah."

"That's what rain looks like. Those heavy streaks mean lots of water coming our way." She looked at the clock above the stove. "Where are those Parkers?"

As if on cue, the back door swung open and the three Parkers came in amid a flurry of wind and dust. Mr. Parker pushed the door closed with both hands. "This storm is a cow tipper for sure," he said.

The image made Jade giggle.

"You think I'm joking?" Mr. Parker was playing it up. "I've seen it happen."

Mrs. Parker gave his arm a gentle hit. "You have not."

Mr. Parker looked as innocent as an angel. "I have indeed! Big old cows lying on their backs with their little hooves pointing up to heaven." He shook his head. "It's a tragic sight."

They gathered around the table and began playing a game of Clue. Roy was guessing Colonel Mustard did it in the library with the wrench when the brunt of the storm hit.

A deep and rumbling roll of thunder wrapped around the house, shaking it good. Lightning flashed through the window, a resounding *crack* pierced the air, and with one flicker, the power went out.

"Poor cows," Mr. Parker said in the pitch-dark.

Everyone laughed.

"I hope the dogs are okay," Jade said.

"Those dogs were born and raised under these Wyoming skies." Aunt Elise turned on one of the LED lanterns. "They are in their houses and their kennels are protected with strong tarps. No need to worry there."

"Let's do candles," Mrs. Parker suggested. "It's more cozy."

Aunt Elise fumbled for a box of matches and turned the lantern off. A single strike brought a light to illuminate her face. She ceremoniously lit five pillar candles.

"Much better," Mrs. Parker said.

Shadows danced on the walls as the golden flames sputtered and glimmered on the table. Jade pulled the unfrosted cake from the kitchen countertop. "I wasn't able to finish it," she said, cutting slices. "It's not perfect."

"Uh-uh-uh." Aunt Elise waved a finger in the air. "It's like I always say, perfect . . ."

Jade, Mr. Parker, Mrs. Parker, and Roy finished the sentence in unison: ". . . Has no personality."

26

Rain pounded, lightning slashed, and thunder roared long into the night. Roy and his parents decided to stay over. Aunt Elise pulled out sleeping bags, quilts, and at least twenty pillows. She pushed aside the living room couch and coffee table and piled the mound of blankets and pillows in the middle of the room. Mrs. Parker moved the candles in from the kitchen and lined them along the windowsill. Jade watched their reflection flicker and shine against the black glass.

Mr. Parker stood at that large living room window, his back to the others. A gash of lightning cut across the sky as the rain kept battering down on the adobe house. "The land lines are down, I'll try my cell." He was attempting to call Angelo and Tilly to be sure they were all right.

Them, and a whole list of other people in town he helped from time to time.

Roy set up two sleeping bags and a mound of pillows on one side of the room. He sat on a sleeping bag and motioned for Jade to sit on the other.

"My mom asked me to enter the Juniper Festival poetry contest with her," Roy said, tucking a pillow behind his head.

"Are you going to do it?"

"I guess so. Sit down, I have a confession to make."

Jade sat. "What kind of confession?"

"Promise you won't be mad." Roy's knee started to bop and bounce.

"What did you do?"

Roy looked over to the window where the adults were counting lightning strikes. "I sent away for my genealogy." He had the goofiest expression. "It's coming, Jade. The proof is on its way."

"Why would I be ups—" Then it hit her. "You used our money from Farley, didn't you?"

"I had no choice."

"It was supposed to be for you-know-who." Jade jerked her head toward Mr. Parker.

"There's still some left. Are you mad at me?"

"I guess not."

"Good, because I'm excited." He was squirming all around that navy-blue sleeping bag.

"But what if . . ." Jade couldn't bring herself to say what she was actually thinking. To ask Roy what he would do if his grand assumptions were proven wrong. "Never mind."

Aunt Elise came away from the window. "It's moving on."

Jade thought the rain seemed as heavy as ever. "How do you know?"

Aunt Elise pointed to Copernicus, who was slinking out from under the couch. "That cat is the best weatherman this side of the moon. If he's showing his face, the worst is behind us."

Copernicus bounded onto a couch cushion, stretched, and yawned. His scratchy tongue curled out like a wave. The rain overhead went from a pounding to a patter and faded out to nothing. Long strands of moonlight sliced through the dark clouds.

"Well," Aunt Elise said, "I guess our impromptu sleepover is canceled."

"We're not going anywhere." Mrs. Parker was making a bed in the middle of the room. "Who has a good ghost story?"

"Did I ever tell you guys about when Butch was haunted by the spirit of an old railroad hand?" Roy asked.

169

They all settled down on the cloud of comforters and pillows. The candlelight was still flickering against the windowpane, casting shadows across the ceiling and walls.

"I don't believe I've heard that one," Aunt Elise said.

Roy began telling his tale of stolen gold and vengeful spirits. Jade climbed into her sleeping bag and listened. It was Roy Parker at his finest.

27

The next day, after the Parkers left and the dog kennels were put back in order, Aunt Elise led Jade to the muddy bank of a creek out behind her property. "Join me in the shade," she said, sitting under a rumpled oak tree.

Jade crossed the backyard, brushed off a spot of earth, and sat down. The dogs all ran into the water, lapping it up and splashing playfully. The storm the night before had made the water a bit deep for Lobo and Genghis Khan, but it was perfect for the others and barely came up to Astro's middle. Once the dogs had taken a good drink, they each found their own piece of shade.

Astro decided his spot was right between Jade and her aunt. His muddy paws wiped across Jade's yellow shorts, his hot breath panted on her cheek, and his heavy fur was shedding, making her legs itch.

Jade loved it.

"Have you ever floated a boat down a creek?" Aunt Elise asked, pulling a bundle of twigs and twine from her cargo-pants pocket.

"Can't say that I have."

"Excellent." Aunt Elise twisted three sticks together with the string, making a perfect triangle, and handed the supplies over to Jade. "Your turn."

Jade tried to copy her aunt, but the triangle turned out more like a crooked, three-armed cross.

"Doesn't matter a bit," Aunt Elise said, helping Jade tie off the corners. "It'll float just the same." She scooted down to the bank's edge and dropped her boat into the murky, lazy water. It was the leftover rain mixed with Wellington's copper dirt. Jade also inched down and plopped her boat in. The sticks bumped and ambled out of sight.

"Is that it?" Jade asked.

"Floating stick boats down the creek is a classic summer pastime around here. You haven't lived until you've tried it."

They each began making another boat. Jade was determined to fashion a proper triangle.

"I hope you're enjoying your vacation so far," Aunt Elise said, her hands busy at work.

Jade kept twisting the sticks. "You were right when you said it would be an adventure."

"Speaking of which, have you finished *Robinson Crusoe*?"

"I read the last chapter this morning."

"And do you still think he should have stayed home?"

"I guess not."

Aunt Elise smiled. "Good. Sometimes people need to step away from what they know in order to find out who they really are."

"Like when you left Philly and moved out here?"

"I suppose." Aunt Elise put the final twist on her boat. "Brenda told me she was able to convince Roy to give the cowboy-poetry contest a shot. That was a nice thought you had."

Jade studied her aunt, who was focused on preparing the next boat, peeling strips of bark from a twig. Jade turned back to her own work. She had to admit, there was something soothing about twisting those brown sticks together and watching them float down the creek.

"Now that you've got the hang of it, we'll send our troubles sailing. Each time you put one of these into the creek, you assign a worry to it and send it sailing away."

Jade gave her aunt a disbelieving look.

"Humor me," Aunt Elise said. "One trouble for each boat. You don't even have to say them out loud. Easy peasy."

"You forgot the lemon-squeezy part," Jade said, untying a crooked corner of her boat.

"What?"

"The saying is easy peasy lemon squeezy. You forgot the lemon-squeezy part."

"Silly me, how could I forget?"

This time Jade's boat was a perfect triangle. She closed her eyes and wondered which trouble to choose. Recently, there seemed to be so many. She had thought it would get easier when she quit working for Farley, but now she was on the outside, worrying about what kind of mischief Roy might be getting himself into over there. Was he really going to steal those art pieces?

"Got one?" Aunt Elise asked.

Jade opened her eyes. "Got one."

"Me, too." Aunt Elise raised her own stick boat.

They went to the water's edge and gently placed the sticks into the current. Jade's boat bumped into a skinny tree root jutting out from the bank but managed to wriggle its way free.

"See?" Aunt Elise said. "That worry wants to be let go. It doesn't like the cramped place you're holding it."

They watched their twigs meander down the muddy

water, bobbing and turning and fading into small specks off in the distance.

"When you decide to let a worry go," Aunt Elise said, still looking down the creek, "it doesn't disappear right away. It kind of fades slowly, like these boats."

Jade thought about that.

"Want to go chase them?" Aunt Elise asked.

"No," Jade said in almost a whisper.

Aunt Elise took a step sideways, closer to Jade. "Me neither."

28

When Monday came rolling around and the sun was shining bright, Aunt Elise was practically skipping through the house. She kept getting more and more excited as the day wore on.

In the afternoon, she said to Jade for the seventeenth time since lunch, "It's really going to happen. There's not a cloud in the sky. Those Boy Scouts will be here in a few hours."

"Do you know what you're going to teach them?"

"I've been studying their handbook online. I'm supposed to teach them how to care for the telescopes and then I made this work sheet where they can learn constellations and planets and even sketch out the movement of the moon."

"These are paying students, right?" Jade asked.

"Every last one of them." Aunt Elise looked out the window again, smiling at the cloudless sky.

"How many are coming?" Jade asked.

"Six boys plus two leaders."

"That's a hundred and twenty dollars!"

"Not counting the fifteen-dollar refreshment fee for your brownies and lemonade."

"Nice." Jade had already baked and frosted the brownies. She only had to finish squeezing the lemons.

"I'm going to kennel the dogs and sweep the front walk. You make the lemonade."

Aunt Elise bounded out the back door, leaving Jade alone in the kitchen with a pile of lemons on the countertop and Copernicus at her feet.

"She sure is excited," Jade said to the cat.

Copernicus rubbed his side against her ankle, purring.

Jade took it as a compliment on her idea to have Aunt Elise teach the classes. "I'm glad you approve," she said, slicing the lemons in half and squeezing their juice into a green plastic pitcher.

Copernicus sat at her heel and meowed, asking for a taste of whatever Jade was making. He had made a habit of noticing when she was in the kitchen and had become fairly diligent in his requests for a sampling.

"Trust me," Jade said, slicing another lemon and digging the seeds out with the tip of her knife, "you won't like this."

Copernicus meowed louder.

Jade put her knife down. "Fine, don't listen to me." She took half a lemon and squeezed a few drops of juice onto the linoleum.

Copernicus stepped over, sniffed, and looked at Jade with a blended expression of disgust and sadness. Like he wasn't sure if he could ever trust her again.

Jade shook her head. "I tried to tell you," she said, followed by, "Stubborn cat."

Copernicus lifted his tail high and stomped out of the kitchen.

As much as a cat could stomp.

Jade finished making the lemonade, watching her aunt out the window above the sink.

Aunt Elise giggled as she swept the walks and kenneled the dogs and double-checked the ladder at the back of the house. Then they had a quick dinner and stood vigil at the end of the driveway, next to the dog statue, as the sun eased down behind the Tetons.

"Any minute now," Aunt Elise said, craning her neck, searching for a pair of headlights coming up the street.

"They'll be here," Jade assured her.

Aunt Elise smiled and nodded, but kept her eyes on the road.

When the van full of boys finally came up the street and stopped at the gate, Aunt Elise let out a burst of laughter, she was so giddy.

She swung open the gate and waved the van up the drive, running in a cloud of red dust behind the back bumper. Looking at it, Jade thought of Astro and Yaz and Lobo running along the side of Aunt Elise's Lincoln Continental that first time she and Aunt Elise were the ones pulling up the long driveway.

When the Scout troop was finally up on the roof, with their attention focused on her, Aunt Elise directed them to find one of the largest constellations in the sky, Draco. She explained how Draco was Latin for *dragon* or *serpent* and skillfully recounted a story about how this particular dragon was placed in the sky to guard the gods' apple orchard and about the time the great warrior Hercules came to fight him. The boys sat in a semicircle, completely captivated by the ancient tale.

Then she pointed out the planets and helped the Scouts fill in their work sheets by lantern light.

After the lesson was finished, the brownies and lemonade

were gone, and the Scouts were on their way home, Jade hooked her arm into her aunt's and said, "Those star stories were amazing."

"Do you think they had a good time?"

"Absolutely," Jade said. "And I bet they'll spread the word and get other troops to come."

"I would like that," Aunt Elise said. "I would like that a whole bunch."

29

The next afternoon, Jade walked through downtown Wellington. Banners zigzagged across almost every street. They fluttered and flipped in the wind, reminding everyone about the upcoming Juniper Festival. The park across from the YMCA was crawling with workers who were busy draping electrical wires and assembling booths. Festival trucks lined the streets, getting ready to set up their portable tilt-a-wheels and the Pirate Coaster.

Jade took it all in.

"The stage will go right there along the back." Sandy from the YMCA came up behind Jade. "You got your cowboy poetry ready?"

"It's my friend entering, not me."

"Last year the winning poem was about the lonely call of a coyote ringing out across the still black of night."

"You remember it?"

"I wrote it."

Worry settled into Jade's gut. She was so certain the Parkers' poem would win the grand prize, she hadn't even considered the competition. "Are you entering again this year?"

"Look," Sandy began, "entering this competition is about more than winning some prize money. It's about celebrating who we are. It's about the earth and animals and what true wealth is. Some of us spend our whole lives thinking about those things." She put a hand on Jade's shoulder. "I'm not saying your friend can't write a poem, but I wouldn't get your hopes too high." Sandy walked away through the park, stepping over wires and around boxes.

Jade began walking back to Aunt Elise's. She was passing in front of Roy's house when Mrs. Parker came sprinting out the door.

"Jade! You're just the person we need." Her eyes were puffy and tear tracks cut through her face powder. "Have you seen Roy?"

"Not today."

Mr. Parker came up the walk to join them. "Has she seen him?"

Mrs. Parker looked down the street—first to the right

and then to the left and then to the right again. "No." The word came out thin and weak.

"Is everything okay?"

Mr. Parker had some papers in his hand and held them out to her. "It couldn't be worse."

Jade took the papers and began thumbing through them. It was the Parker genealogy Roy had sent away for. "I was worried about this."

"You knew?" Mrs. Parker asked. "Why would you let him do something so foolish? It was fine as long as he was pretending to be related to Butch Cassidy. It made him happy. But sending away for proof is asking for trouble."

"He had already sent for it when he told me," Jade said. "I was hoping there might be a chance . . ."

Mrs. Parker threw her arms in the air. "Do we look like cowboy stock?"

"Roy does."

"Well, we're not. Our family is from Detroit." Mrs. Parker sat down on the sidewalk and dropped her head into her hands. "We told him, but Roy couldn't accept it, so we let him believe what he wanted. I told myself I was supporting him. I thought it was what good moms do."

Mr. Parker sat down next to his wife and put his arm around her. "That *is* what good moms do, Brenda. Don't question yourself for one minute."

"Have you looked over at Farley's ranch?" Jade asked. "He's probably there."

"No," Mrs. Parker said, lifting the hem of her flowing blouse and dabbing her eyes. "He's not there. That's how I knew he was missing. He didn't show up for work." Her words grew heavy as she said, "He even had a chance to shoe horses today and he didn't go."

"For real?" Jade was surprised. The Roy Parker she knew would have missed Christmas to shoe horses. She fiddled with the genealogy papers. "When did these come?"

"It must have been yesterday when I forgot to bring in the mail. He was so moody last night, but I thought it was because he didn't want to work on the Juniper Festival poem. When I got up this morning, I assumed he had already gone to Farley's. Then I got a call around ten saying he never showed for work. We waited a couple of hours, but he didn't come home, and then William found these papers on his bedroom floor. I've called everywhere, looked everywhere." She dropped her face into her hands again and said, "I'm so worried about him."

Jade folded the papers lengthwise. "Don't be. Wherever he is, I'm sure he's fine."

"How can he be fine when he's lost everything he's ever dreamed of? When he's lost his very self?"

"Has he?" Jade asked.

"We're not the family he needed us to be." Mrs. Parker looked down the street, her eyes glazed over. "Poor child," she whispered so Jade could barely hear.

Jade had a thought. "I might know where he is."

Both Parkers perked up at that. "Where?" they asked in unison.

"Don't worry." Jade started down the walkway. "I'll find him."

Mr. Parker hollered after her, "And bring him home or call us if you do."

"I will," Jade said. "I promise."

30

Jade pressed her face against the glass of the County Hardware store. She looked in every angle of window and banged on both the front and back doors, hollering out Roy's name.

He wasn't there.

She sat on the curb, under the words *Summer is here!* on the window and tried to think of where he could have gone or how he must be feeling. Eventually she found herself walking down the street toward the Hammer and Nail.

She saw his boots first, dangling from a high branch in the tree across the street from Farley's store.

"Hey," she said, looking into the tree.

Roy didn't answer. He just kept swinging his feet.

"You gonna make me climb up there?"

Nothing.

"Fine." Jade positioned her shoe on the knothole and hoisted herself up. "Because I'm a pro at this."

Roy let out a soft huff.

"I am! I had an amazing teacher."

Another huff.

She kept her focus on him, double-checking each foothold. "A pain in the neck, but still amazing."

As she got closer, she noticed him wipe his cheek with his palm.

"Are you impressed?" she said when she reached the thick branch and sat next to him.

Roy shrugged. Jade started swinging her legs in unison with her friend. She didn't look over at him and she didn't say anything for the longest time. Finally, she found her words. "I saw the papers." She knew to let that sink in for a minute before adding, "Does it matter?"

Roy turned to Jade with a baffled look. "Detroit?" he said, as if it was the most bizarre place in the world. "I can't believe it's true."

Jade decided to try a different approach. "I heard you didn't go to Farley's today. Did you know they were shoeing horses?"

"Does *that* matter?"

"It does to the Roy I know. To the Roy who doesn't care what people think about him and who has dreams bigger than anyone I've ever met. I like that Roy."

Another huff, this one a little sharper.

Jade looked across the street. The Hammer and Nail's parking lot was half full and shoppers were coming and going at a pretty regular pace. "Guess they found the fish."

"Doesn't matter," Roy said. "I've moved on to bigger and better plans."

"Like?"

"Like selling Farley's junk on eBay. I've been doing some research and it turns out you were right. He's got some really valuable pieces. That bronco statue was made by this guy named Remington and is worth about thirty-five."

"Hundred?"

"Thousand," Roy said. He tugged a leaf from one of the branches and began shredding it. "Thirty-five thousand smackeroos. If I can pull it off, it'd be a job for the record books."

"Stealing from Farley won't make you more of a cowboy."

Roy was dismissive. "You don't know anything."

"I know you're not a criminal, which is what taking that statue will make you. How would you even explain getting that kind of money to your parents? There's got to be a better way to help them. What about your entry for the cowboy-poetry contest? Aunt Elise says your mom is happy as a pig in mud to be working with you." Jade forced a laugh, trying to lighten the mood. "Who says things like that besides Aunt Elise?"

"It's over," Roy said.

"No it's not. It's in four days and we're counting on you. How close are you and your mom to being finished?"

"I said I'm not doing it." Roy spit the words out like darts.

"You're giving up?" Jade struggled against her frustration. She would never get through to Roy if she gave in to her impulse to start yelling. "Listen," she said, soft and easy, "you are more than a piece of paper. You can be anything you choose and it doesn't come from outside of you. It comes from here." She placed her pointer finger on his heart. "Of all the people I know, I think you'd be the one to understand that."

"You must not know many people then," Roy mumbled.

That was it. The irritation simmered up and spilled out of her mouth. "You need to get over yourself."

Roy turned his head to the side and wiped his cheek again. He said nothing.

Jade let out an annoyed breath and started climbing

down the tree, grumbling the entire way. When she reached the ground, she put her fists on her hips and hollered up at Roy. "Butch Cassidy would never quit like that!"

Roy shot back, "That's fine because I'm not related to him. I'm from a line of stupid builders in Detroit!" He ran his forearm along his runny nose and looked over to Farley's store again. "You don't get it," he said. "It hurts."

All the frustration drained out of Jade. "I know it does," she said. "And you have a choice." She thought she could see Roy's jaw flinch as he recognized his own words. "You can cowboy up and do the right thing by helping your mom. Or you can just lie there and bleed."

31

Jade went to Roy's house and told his parents where he was, and then retraced her route from the morning so she could take a long walk before returning to the dog ranch. She passed the YMCA and the park where the festival was shaping up. She zigzagged down a side street she knew would take her by the Wells Fargo bank. She strolled past the wide front yards that spread out from the center of town, waving at Angelo in his rocker, and she felt an overwhelming relief as she came up to Aunt Elise's house and saw Astro's broad black nose prodding out from a square of the chain-link fence.

He politely stepped back, allowing her to open the gate. "Hey, boy," she said, running a hand along his back.

Aunt Elise came down the driveway. "How are you?"

She asked it in a way that let Jade know the Parkers must have called and explained what had happened.

"I'm okay."

Aunt Elise guided Jade across the yard and into the house. "Do you want to talk?" Aunt Elise said.

"No. I think I'll go lie down for a while."

"That's fine."

When Aunt Elise called Jade for dinner, she said, "I hope you're hungry. I made meatballs."

"Buffalo?" Jade asked.

"Sorry," Aunt Elise said, pulling out a kitchen chair and offering it to Jade. "I was out of buffalo so I went with ostrich."

"You're kidding, right?"

Aunt Elise smiled. "Yes, I'm kidding. You're going to have to settle for boring old beef tonight. But I'm fairly certain I ruined the rice—if that helps at all." She reached over and turned on the corner fan, sending a whirling breeze to ruffle the stars and planets overhead. Jade knew it was in honor of Roy's heartache. "One scoop or two?" Aunt Elise was dipping a ladle into the Crock-Pot of meatballs and sauce.

Jade thought of how much her aunt's cooking had improved over the past few weeks. "Two."

They ate dinner without a word, the glittered and bright art twisting above them. When the last plate was washed and the counters had been wiped down, Aunt Elise asked, "So what's your plan?"

"You expect me to make this better for Roy?"

"Who else?"

Jade hung up the dish towel she was using and went outside to think about the situation. She crossed the backyard, followed by a line of dogs. She ran her fingers through the long grass, kicked some rocks, and peered up into the sky. Before long, she found herself under the rumpled oak by the creek bed. Astro nudged his head up under her arm.

"Got any ideas, boy?" Jade asked, sitting down on the grassy slope.

Astro *harrumphed* and sat down next to her. The other dogs followed suit, tongues wagging in the evening heat.

Jade noticed some leftover sticks and string off to the side, where her aunt had left them a couple of days before. Without thought, she took the sticks and began twisting them into a triangle. Astro pushed out his front paws, lay down, and looked at Jade with his dark watery eyes as if to say, *Tell me all about it.*

"Why did he have to send away for his genealogy?" she began, working her boat. "He was plenty happy living with his imaginary ancestors. Why did he have to go and ruin it?"

Astro kept his eyes fixed on Jade and gave the smallest nod.

"Your real life is never as good as what your imagination can create," Jade said, and, as she did, Astro puffed out a heavy breath and shook his head sharply.

Jade pressed her lips together. "Are you disagreeing with me?" As if to test her theory, she said it again. "Your real life is never as good as what your imagination can create."

Astro shook his head once more. Sharp and decisive. Full of surety.

Jade didn't know what to think about that. She finished her boat, inched down to the creek that was now just a trickle, and dropped it in. "This one is yours," she said to Roy. "You've got to let that burden go." The sticks moved slowly, but eventually worked their way down and out of sight. Jade pulled her knees up, crossed her arms, and rested her chin.

Lobo waddled to her side, teeth jutting up over his lip. Jade tugged on his stumpy tail and tried to keep thinking about how to help Roy. Nothing was coming to mind.

Dusty evening melted into twilight before Jade gave up and went back into the house. When she came through the door, Aunt Elise looked at her with a hopeful expression.

Jade shook her head. "There's nothing we can do. I told

him he was more than a stack of papers. I even floated a stick boat down the creek for him."

"You can't float someone else's worries away."

"I'm at a loss."

Aunt Elise put aside her book and stood up. "Let's ask the stars."

Jade loved her aunt. She had come to appreciate—even enjoy—her eccentricities over the past two weeks. But Jade was also a realist. She knew they had run into a brick wall and Roy had to figure out the situation for himself. "It's hopeless," she said.

"It's never hopeless. You're just not listening."

"Listening to what?"

Aunt Elise lowered her voice. "The promptings."

Jade started to walk away, but Aunt Elise grabbed her arm. "Let's go listen together." Aunt Elise pulled Jade back through the kitchen, out the door, and to the ladder.

"I don't think that—" Jade began to protest.

Aunt Elise raised a finger to her lips and then pointed to her ear as if to say, *No talking, just listening.*

Jade clamped her mouth shut and followed her aunt onto the roof. She thought the idea was absurd, but she still followed.

The evening was deepening. A sliver of moon hung over

the Tetons in the distance and a patchwork of black clouds filled the sky.

"I doubt we'll see many stars tonight," Jade said, looking at those clouds.

Aunt Elise did the finger-to-her-mouth-and-then-ear thing again.

Jade stretched out on a beach lounger and waited as night fully eased over the valley. Aunt Elise was on the lounger to Jade's left. After about an hour of lying in the dark, Jade said, "How long are we going to stay up here?"

"For as long as it takes," Aunt Elise whispered. "Are you thinking about possibilities?"

Jade had to admit she wasn't. She had been watching the occasional faint star shining through the clouds and thinking about how much time had passed. It had been a long hour, but it was clear her aunt was in no hurry to go anywhere, so Jade kept watching the sky.

To pass the time, she began revisiting her day—the festival trucks lined up downtown and the banners draped across the streets. Sandy and her smug confidence about winning the poetry contest again. She thought about the panic in Mrs. Parker's face when she ran out to meet Jade and the miserable look in Mr. Parker's eyes when he handed her that stack of genealogy papers. How he knew his son was hurting.

It all played out in her head.

Finally, she thought about sitting on the creek bed and wishing away Roy's sorrow with a simple triangle of sticks. How Astro had looked at her and seemed to understand every word she said. How he had even disagreed with her, or at least gave that impression.

Astro.

That loving beast.

Jade breathed in the night air and thought about how much she adored that dog.

And in those moments of thought about genealogy papers and heartache and Astro, Jade's answer came.

It nearly took her breath away, the idea was so clear and perfect.

"I know what we need to do," she said, sitting up, filled with light and wonder, and amazement that Aunt Elise's listening plan had actually worked. A laugh bubbled out. "I do! I know exactly what Roy needs."

Aunt Elise reached over. "See?" she said. "The stars always answer."

32

Jade needed to speak to Roy's parents alone, but that wasn't a problem. When she went over the following day, she learned he had shut himself up in his bedroom and refused to come out—even when his mom made her out-of-this-world cinnamon rolls.

"We'll visit in the front yard," Mrs. Parker said, wanting to be certain of their privacy.

Once they were a ways from the house, Jade began to explain her plan. "Mr. Parker, how much do you know about your family history?"

He shoved his fists into the pockets of his brown bathrobe. "Not much beyond a generation or two."

"What about that box of journals and pictures you got when your dad passed on?" Mrs. Parker said. "Is there much information there?"

"Might be," he said.

"Do you have the papers Roy sent for?" Jade asked.

"I have most of them; why?"

"Well, I was out by the creek talking to Astro." She paused a moment, understanding the unusual nature of what she had said. The Parkers were not fazed in the least.

"Go on," Mr. Parker said.

"And I said something about how the real world is never as good as what our imagination can come up with and he did the weirdest thing. He looked right at me and shook his head, like he was disagreeing with me."

Mr. Parker let out a small laugh. "Crazy dog."

"I didn't think much of it at the time," Jade went on, "but later, when Aunt Elise and I were listening to the stars . . ." She paused. Still, again, the Parkers seemed to accept what she said without hesitation. "I thought, what if Astro's right? What if Roy's real family line could be as interesting as the one he's imagined all these years?"

"I don't think any old pictures I might be able to dig up will compare to Butch Cassidy," Mr. Parker said. "He's an American legend!"

"You might be surprised," Jade said. "My dad tells this story about how his distant great-uncle fought right alongside Ulysses S. Grant in the Civil War and later served under his presidency."

"Is that so?"

"He even has a Medal of Honor this guy supposedly earned. What I'm saying is there could be all sorts of stories in your own family history. Maybe teaching Roy more about who he *is* will stop him from being so sad about who he *isn't.*"

Mrs. Parker fluttered a hand over her mouth. "That's an exceptional idea!"

Mr. Parker went into his work shed, stepped past his glass-blowing equipment, and went to a cardboard box shoved in the corner. "I've never even looked in here," he said, pulling out a stack of pictures.

"I did," Mrs. Parker said. "When it first came. It's all from your father's side."

"The Parker line," Jade said, knowing it was perfect for her plan. "He may not be related to the famous Roy Parker, but maybe we can show him some other Parkers who were just as great."

All three sat around the box, taking one piece of paper out at a time. They looked at pictures and read the lines printed on the back: *Horace at Lake Erie* or *Ginny with the cat.*

It didn't look promising.

They studied old letters and newspaper clippings and tried to sort the information into family-group piles. From what Jade could see, there were generations of records there. Years and years of people's lives reduced to a mess of paper, scattered across the workshop floor. She wondered if that was all she would be someday: a picture at the bottom of a cardboard box.

"Did you know any of these people?" she asked, organizing some black-and-white photos by dates.

"A few," Mr. Parker said. "I knew my grandparents of course, but they never talked much of my great-grandparents. I think my great-grandfather worked for the railroad. That's about all I knew of him."

Jade got excited for a second. "Was he ever working on a train that got robbed by the Wild Bunch?" The Wild Bunch, Roy had repeatedly told her, was the name of Butch Cassidy's gang.

"I think he spent more time building the rails than riding them," Mr. Parker said.

"Oh."

They went back to reading letters and sorting piles. Then Mr. Parker stood up. "There's nothing here," he said. "Just regular people living regular lives." He dropped a brown leather journal back into the box and went inside.

Mrs. Parker forced a smile. "Good folks," she said. "But no Medals of Honor in the Parker line. Thanks for trying, Jade. It was a nice thought."

"Do you mind if I stay longer?" Jade asked.

Mrs. Parker let out a quiet groan as she stood up. "I'm afraid it's more pictures of Horace at the lake or Ginny with the cat, but you're welcome to keep looking."

"Thanks."

Mrs. Parker went inside, leaving Jade alone. She picked up a photograph of a young boy on a tricycle and tried to imagine what life for him might have been like. He wore red shorts, suspenders, and a miniature sailor's hat. She flipped the picture over: *William, 1976.* It was Roy's dad. Jade set the picture aside and pulled out another, this one black-and-white and of a woman standing by a Cadillac. She flipped it over: *Rita's new ride, 1953.*

Then she pulled that brown leather journal out of the box. It belonged to someone named George J. Parker and the dates were all from the '20s and '30s:

June 26, 1924
Began construction on the Detroit Institute
of Arts (DIA) today. Lucky to have

*the work, though I'd prefer to have my
paintings featured inside instead of just
laying the bricks. Maybe someday.*

Another Parker artist, Jade thought. She flipped ahead in the book and read a different page:

*August 2, 1934
Lulu made soup. It was delicious.*

Jade shut the journal. Maybe Mr. and Mrs. Parker were right. These records were about good, hardworking people but there was nothing special about any of them. At least, nothing that would pull Roy out of his sorrow. She stacked the photos into the box and began to shove it back into the corner, but couldn't bring herself to do it. Something about that seemed disrespectful to those people. Like they didn't matter. Instead, she lifted the box onto Mr. Parker's workbench.

"I guess that's what I get for listening to a dog," she said.

A voice cut in behind her. "Was it Lobo or Yaz?"

Roy.

"You feeling better?"

He lifted a shoulder. "So what did the dog say?"

Jade glanced back to the box. "Nothing."

"That's because dogs don't actually talk." He whirled a finger at his temple.

Jade knew he was teasing and was happy he felt good enough to make fun.

Roy pulled a pair of orange tennis shoes from a pile of shoes by the door, sat down, and started working them onto his feet.

"No cowboy boots?"

"Someone recently told me I have to get over that."

"What I said," Jade clarified, "is that you have to get over feeling sorry for yourself and learn to be okay with the truth."

Roy jerked his head up. Everything about his face looked tired and worn down. His eyes were deep sunken pits with dark lines smeared underneath. "Maybe it's time we both start living our truths. You quit writing papers about summer adventures you've never had and I'll come to terms with the fact that I'm nobody."

"Did Aunt Elise tell you about my binder?"

"I have my ways."

"Fine. So I made up a couple of stories. Who cares? But you're wrong about being nobody."

"No I'm not. I even have the paperwork to prove it." He went back to tying his shoes.

Jade was out of patience. "I wonder why the people at Genealogy.com didn't stamp a red A for average on your pedigree chart. Or even better, a big N for nitwit." She didn't wait for Roy to answer. She left him there in his dad's workshop and went home.

33

Everyone was gearing up for Wellington's Juniper Festival, just two days away. People put twinkle lights in their trees and fixed mini Wyoming state flags to their car antennas. The flag was blue with red trim and a big white buffalo in the middle. Jade couldn't look at it without remembering Aunt Elise's stew and feeling guilty.

"How big are the fireworks?" Jade asked her aunt as they wrapped streamers around the dog statue and threaded them through the chain-link fence at the end of Aunt Elise's driveway.

"The ones we'll set off here or the ones at the festival?"

Jade stopped threading. "Wyoming allows private fireworks?"

"Sure."

"Even after the Fourth of July?"

Realization came into Aunt Elise's eyes. "Wyoming allows them year-round. I forgot how restrictive Philly is when it comes to fireworks. You've probably not had the chance to have anything other than sparklers." She was overflowing with excitement. "Let's go right now. There are two stands out on the county line. You can have your pick! We'll get fountains and those neat twisty things . . ." She was speedily threading the last bits of streamers through the fence. "And the spinning flowers that change colors as they shoot across the pavement. Those are my favorite." Her long, thin eyebrows wiggled from under her bangs. "Let your old auntie take care of everything. Your only job is to relax and have a good time. No worrying allowed."

More than anything in that moment, Jade wanted to let go of the heaviness she had been feeling and have a freewheeling fireworks extravaganza. "Okay," she said. "But only if we get some of those strobes that flash superbright."

Much to Jade's surprise, Astro loved fireworks. He sat down next to her folding camp chair and watched each fantastic spray of light with intense eagerness. It was as if he was trying to figure out how so much power came from such a small package. He'd watch the display, shake his head, and slap his tongue across his lips in disbelief. Then he'd look to Aunt Elise as if to say, *Do it again!*

The other dogs weren't as interested. They huddled down in their houses, bothered by the loud *pops* and *snaps* Jade and her aunt were setting off at the end of the drive. All except Genghis Khan, that is. He sat on the porch with an air of disinterest, refusing to be sent running.

Jade looked up into the night, mesmerized by how the spray of firework lights seemed to mingle with the low-hanging stars, as if they were partners coming together in a dance. It was extraordinary.

"I gave Brenda and William a call, but they didn't feel right coming without Roy." Aunt Elise was lining up three pillar fireworks for another one of her triple-threat displays.

"And he's still pouting?"

Aunt Elise lit the wicks with her punk and stepped back quickly. One, two, three . . . purple and white sparks shot up into the night, whizzing and popping. "There comes a time in everyone's life when they have to decide if they're going to accept themselves as they are or keep wishing they were someone else." She sat down in the chair next to Jade. "Roy's time came sooner than most, is all."

Jade pulled three more pillar fireworks from the pile off

to the side. She removed the finished cylinders and stacked the new ones. "Did you have that time?"

"Sure I did." Aunt Elise tilted her head back and reached for some long-lost memory. "I graduated from law school at the top of my class and made partner at one of the largest firms in Philly in less than three years."

"That's good, right?"

"It was everything I wanted. I was in the city of my dreams, making a good living, but after a while I started to realize I didn't have much of a life. The hours were horrendous and the stress was robbing me of even the smallest measure of peace. Well, one morning, I was going through some old pictures and came across one of myself from years before. Only, it looked like someone else—someone happy. More than anything, I wanted to be that person again." Aunt Elise closed her eyes, lingering over faded thoughts. "That's about the time a friend invited me out to Wyoming for a much-needed vacation. I traded the corporate ladder for the one that goes up to my roof and, for me, it was the right choice. I couldn't keep trying to be something I wasn't."

"But Roy *is* a cowboy," Jade said. "Through and through. Why can't he see he doesn't need any paperwork to prove it?"

Aunt Elise started gathering bits of firework trash from

the driveway, shoving it into a bag. "This isn't about Roy finding the cowboy inside, Jade. It's about him finding the hero inside. He loves Butch Cassidy for all those Robin Hood stories, not for his belt buckles and boots. Heck, no one in Wyoming needs an excuse to wear those things. They're commonplace. Roy clung to them for what they symbolized. For what he hoped they would help him become." Then she added, "That's a lot to lose."

Jade knew her aunt was right. It was the whole reason she had spent two hours sifting through that box of genealogy paperwork in the Parkers' workshop—she was trying to find a real hero Roy could cling to.

Instead, she had only found pictures of cats and journal entries about good soup.

34

On Saturday, Jade and her aunt filled their pockets with quarters for the rides, slathered on sunscreen, and walked over to Wellington's Juniper Festival. Cotton-candy and snow-cone vendors were on every corner. Men walked around carrying giant sticks with peanut bags and those foam Cat in the Hat hats dangling from nails.

"Let's load up on beads now, before they're sold out," Aunt Elise said, waving down a salesman. "I love wearing these beaded necklaces. Then we'll hit the Pirate Coaster." It was like she was eight years old and at her first festival.

"When is the poetry reading?" Jade asked.

Aunt Elise paid the vendor ten dollars for ten plastic beaded necklaces and slid half of them around her neck and the other half around Jade's neck. They were in the state's colors—red, white, and blue. "In about forty minutes. I'm so excited for Brenda!"

Roy's mom had finished the poem, even though Roy wasn't interested in helping. Jade knew she had done it so everyone wouldn't be disappointed, but Jade doubted the poem would be what it needed to be. She kept thinking about what Sandy from the YMCA had said—how people took the contest seriously and how a person couldn't fake love for those images. Could Roy's mom write about lonely wolves and wide-open skies?

"Is he coming?" Jade was referring to Roy.

"He'll do what he needs to do."

"Which is come and support his mom, right?"

"If he's ready, he'll come. If he's not, he won't. You never know what will happen—which reminds me, I have two more stargazing bookings. Tuesday night is another group of Boy Scouts—you were right about getting referrals from the last event—and next Saturday I'll host Sandy and her family. They wanted to try it out." Aunt Elise straightened Jade's necklaces. "I'm sorry you won't be here for them."

"It's all right," Jade said. "I like that you'll keep hosting classes after I go home."

"I can't believe our time together is almost finished. Tomorrow is our last full day."

"It's gone by so fast," Jade said.

Aunt Elise's mouth sagged down for a moment before she pulled it up into a grin and asked, "Are you interested in coming back next summer?"

"Absolutely," Jade said.

"Excellent! And how about we go hiking tomorrow? That would be a nice way to celebrate your last day."

"Up Grand Teton?" Jade asked nervously.

Aunt Elise laughed. "Heavens no, that's a ten-hour hike. It would take you two or three summers to train for a hike of that level. No Grand Teton this time. They have over two hundred miles of trails in that area, something for every level. Let's take it easy tomorrow. Maybe we'll go on the Cottonwood Creek trail. It has the most breathtaking meadows, which should be bursting with summer wild-flowers this time of year."

Jade was relieved. "That sounds pretty."

Aunt Elise stood on her tippy toes, trying to look over the crowd. "What's the line like at the coaster?"

Jade looked. "Medium."

"Let's go." Aunt Elise started pushing Jade through the multitude of people, weaving by families and dodging baby strollers. "If we hurry, we can ride it before we have to go over to the pavilion for the reading."

Jade wasn't exactly a roller-coaster type of girl, but this

one looked small enough and her aunt seemed so eager to share the experience. When they got to the line, she watched the pirate-ship cars jerk and wobble along the portable rails. "So they set this up with a couple of screws and wire?" she asked, watching a little boy jostle within the car as it whipped around a corner.

Aunt Elise brushed a hand through the air. "It's two feet off the ground. Even if it completely collapsed, how far would you fall?"

"Still . . ."

Aunt Elise stepped up to the front of the line, paid her fifty cents, and all but skipped into the fenced area and onto a coaster car. Jade followed. Once she was crammed into the car next to her aunt, with the metal bar—hot and sweaty from the day's use—pulled down across her thighs, Aunt Elise leaned over. "Can you feel your blood pumping?"

"I guess."

Aunt Elise nodded. "That's how you know you're alive."

As she said those words, the freckled-faced coaster worker pushed a big red button, sending them off with a solid jerk.

It bobbed and bounced at first, building up speed on the straightaway and then tossed Jade into her aunt as it flung them around the corner and up a small incline.

"Wheee!" Aunt Elise was waving both hands high above her head. She had completely surrendered to the moment. "Whooo!"

Forty-two seconds later, another jerk brought them to a stop in front of that freckle-faced festival worker.

"You have to admit," Aunt Elise said as she climbed out, "that was a good time."

Jade's heart was flopping and thumping around her chest like a fish out of water, but her aunt had been right about one thing: there was no question she was alive.

Aunt Elise looked at her watch. "Time to scoot over to the pavilion if we want good seats."

They stopped and got giant snow cones on the way and then met Mr. Parker, Angelo, and Tilly down on the first row.

"Is she nervous?" Aunt Elise asked Mr. Parker.

"As a cat in a car wash," he said.

Angelo cleared his throat. "She's all spunk, that one. She'll do fine."

"Have any of you heard the poem?" Tilly asked.

Mr. Parker shook his head. "She's kept it under wraps. Says it's top secret." He flicked a finger to his lips when he said *top secret*.

"But it's about Western stuff, right?" Jade asked.

Aunt Elise put a reassuring hand on Jade's knee. "I'm sure it is."

Jade sat up straight and looked around for Roy.

The MC, a tall, knobby man with a hat brim wider than his whole self, cleared his throat into the microphone and began the contest. He announced they would follow the written program, which put Brenda Parker in the number-seven-out-of-nine spot.

Up first was a weary-looking cowboy, older than the hills. The moment he stepped onto the stage, Jade knew he had something to say. Something wise and meaningful. Something nostalgic.

He spoke in rich tones about the life he loved so much and about a certain time on a cattle drive when a baby calf got lost and no one could figure out where it went. He told about how he sent that calf's mama out after him and how she went directly to her child, lost and wandering in the woods.

The poem nearly brought a tear to Jade's eye. It was a story about an old cow, but the way he told it you knew it was about much more. It was about things like fear and love. Things like family.

Jade pushed the red plastic straw through her snow cone. Her visions of a fat blue ribbon and big check faded with every new poet that took the stage.

They were real cowboys. Every last one of them. Even Sandy came out wearing a suede vest and boots and a pretty straw hat. Her poem for this year was about a dark mountain shadow crawling across the land at dusk, and it was perfect.

And then it was Mrs. Parker's turn. She swept onto the stage the same way she had breezed across Aunt Elise's rooftop Jade's first night in Wellington—flowing rainbow chiffon and smiling entirely too wide. There was none of the stoicism, none of the thoughtful gazes out across the crowd. It went without saying that she wasn't wearing anything close to the appropriate attire for such an occasion. Jade's heart sank.

"I'd like to dedicate this poem to my son, Roy Parker," she said. The microphone squeaked and squawked as she adjusted it to her height. She raised her arms out to the side and began:

> *"Tell me of a cowboy's heart*
> *A gentle spirit under unyielding skies*
> *Tell me of his courage strong*
> *A brazen faith that never dies.*
>
> *"A cowboy doesn't shun the fight*
> *He dares to live, to make a stand*

And when you feel you've lost your way
He reaches out and takes your hand.

"A cowboy is that faithful friend
With kindness from the very start
You'll find this if you dare to look
Within a cowboy's loving heart."

When the last word fell from her lips, everyone started cheering and clapping. Jade nearly toppled her snow cone in the bustle. She looked over to Aunt Elise, who was about to bust clean open with joy and then over to Mr. Parker, who was dabbing his eyes with a napkin and then over to Angelo, who suddenly, and quite amazingly, had Roy standing next to him. Roy was looking down and fiddling with the back handle of Angelo's wheelchair. Jade scooted past the others and over to him. "Didn't you love that?"

Roy nodded, his face still down.

Jade touched his arm. "She may not know a lot about Western life, but she knows you."

"Yep," Roy said, looking up. "I guess she does."

35

Brenda Parker didn't get the twenty-five-hundred-dollar grand prize. She got third place, which was a yellow ribbon and two free rides on the Pirate Coaster. Mrs. Parker offered the tickets to Angelo and Tilly.

"Don't you think we're too old for this sort of thing?" Tilly asked.

"Not at all," Angelo said, taking the tickets and wheeling himself into the line.

Jade found her way to Mrs. Parker's side. "I loved your poem. Too bad you didn't win the prize money for your store."

Mrs. Parker pinned her yellow prize ribbon on her blouse. "No need to worry about that. William has two job interviews this coming week. Something will turn up."

"It absolutely will," Mr. Parker said, reaching an arm around Roy's neck and pulling him in playfully. "Glad you decided to come."

"I wouldn't have missed it," Roy said. "Not really."

"Are you feeling better?" Mrs. Parker asked.

"I got looking in that box of stuff in dad's workshop. You know, the one Jade was poking through the other day?"

Mrs. Parker tilted her head. "The one full of cat pictures?"

"There was other stuff in there, too," Roy said. "Did you know we had a relative who made really good soup?"

"Lulu?" Jade asked, remembering.

"She was married to this George guy who was my long-ago uncle. One day he took his lunch break and saw this kid sitting on a bench. Come to find out, the kid was all alone because the economy was struggling and jobs were hard to find so both his parents had left town to look for work. Can you imagine leaving a fourteen-year-old boy all to himself in a big city?"

"Goodness, no," Mrs. Parker said.

"I guess that's what families had to do in those hard times," Roy went on. "The first week or so, this Uncle George of ours sat next to the boy and shared his soup. After that, he invited the boy home and gave him a place to sleep at night. Took him off the streets without a second thought. I mean, who does that?"

"A Parker does that," Roy's dad said.

"Later," Roy continued, "this boy talked Uncle George's wife, Lulu, into opening a soup kitchen out of her backyard and they fed families and migrant workers and anyone who needed a hand up. That's what Uncle George and Aunt Lulu liked to call it, a hand up, not a handout."

"How remarkable," Mrs. Parker said.

"That's not the half of it. I found this letter that Lulu wrote to George describing why she decided to marry him. She wrote about an experience in their town with a boy named Harold. Harold had special needs. I guess some of the kids gave him a hard time, but most ignored him. Anyway, one day George came to pick Lulu up in his truck and take her into town, which was kind of a big deal if you lived out in the country." Roy was on fire, bobbing and bouncing and shining bright. "Lulu gets in the pickup truck and off they go. All of a sudden, she notices Harold walking along the side of the road. Without saying anything, George pulls over, rolls down his window, and says, 'Get in, Harold. We're goin' to town.' Just like that!" Roy snapped his fingers. "'Get in, Harold.' That's when Lulu knew George was a keeper because he was kind to Harold when no one else would be."

"Cool story," Jade said.

"It's not a story." Roy seemed annoyed. "It's who we are." Then he linked it all together: "Did I ever tell you about the time Butch Cassidy returned a horse to a little boy?" He launched into the story before Jade even had a chance to answer. He told about how a member of the Wild Bunch rode into camp one afternoon on a newly stolen horse and how he bragged about stealing it from a boy in town. "Can you imagine what Butch did when he heard that?" Roy shook his head and giggled before he told about how Butch had pulled out his gun and ridden with him all the way back into town to return the horse to the boy. "Then he made him walk the four miles back to camp. Butch Cassidy was someone who helped those who couldn't help themselves. Butch cared about the little guy when no one else did." Roy turned to his parents. "And George Parker was exactly that same kind of man."

Both Mr. and Mrs. Parker were standing with their jaws scraping the pavement. Mr. Parker regained his composure and said, "Is that so?"

Roy gave a single nod. "Sure is."

"And you got all of this from that cardboard box?"

"It got me thinking," Roy said. "If Butch Cassidy was in Wellington today, he'd probably volunteer to build a new wheelchair ramp for Angelo or put up a pen for the Wilsons' calf. He'd probably do it on his own time and not even charge the folks who couldn't afford to pay."

Mrs. Parker was glowing. "Who needs the grand prize when you have boys like this?"

Standing there, Jade could see Roy had finally found whatever it was he had lost. Only this time it was better, because it was real.

36

After the coaster ride, Mr. and Mrs. Parker took Angelo and Tilly home. Tilly looked a little shaken from being jostled around the tracks, but Angelo was radiant. Aunt Elise scrounged a handful of quarters from the bottom of her purse and held them up to Jade and Roy. "Shall we take one last ride?"

Roy shook his head. "I'm in the mood for some cotton candy."

"Me, too," Jade said.

"You two go on, then." Aunt Elise jumped back into the coaster line. "I'll meet you at home, Jade."

Jade and Roy wandered over to the food trucks, squinting against the bright afternoon sun. Blue sky stretched tight and wide overhead. They had only been in the cotton-candy line for a minute when Farley came across the park, taking long strides right up to Roy.

He dipped his chin and tugged at the brim of his hat in greeting. "We've missed seeing you over at the ranch," he said to Roy.

"I haven't been feeling well." Roy was shifting in his boots.

"I understand," Farley said. His tone told Jade that he knew what Roy had been through. "But I want to say that you're welcome to come back to work whenever you're feeling better. Stuart said you are one of the best trainees he's ever worked with. I've seen you with him. It's effortless the way you ride." Then he did that hat-tug thing again, smiled at Jade, and walked away.

Roy ordered one large cotton candy to share and found a seat on the bumper of a concession truck.

They peeled threads of the sticky pink treat and melted it across their tongues. When the candy was all gone and only the paper cone was left, Jade began picking at a faded bumper sticker on the concession truck. It read: *Pray for Whirled Peas*.

"That was nice of Farley," she said. "Maybe he's not such a bad guy after all."

"Kip Farley is never going to make my list of favorite

225

people," Roy said, "but I think it's time to let it go. He probably didn't deserve those fish heads. And you were right about the whole eBay thing. I am better than that."

"So you're not going through with it?"

"No. I decided to leave the Boys and Girls Club donation pledge at fifty dollars, too. I was talking to my parents and it turns out my dad really wants to try something new, so maybe the store shutting down wasn't so terrible. And they said if I do go back to Farley's ranch, any money I make can be saved for a plane ticket to Philadelphia. If you're interested in having a visitor, that is."

"Are you kidding me? I'd love to show you Philly! I could take you to Franklin Square and the Benjamin Franklin Bridge and we can go to the city library—it's massive— and we can stop at Mr. Yee's market and get candy bars on the way home. You'll love it." Jade went back to picking at the bumper sticker. She focused intently on the sun-bleached letters, running a finger along the word *Peas* and working her thumbnail under a corner, separating it from the rusted chrome. "Will you keep the nickname Roy?"

"I'll have to give that some thought," Roy said. "I think I'll keep it for now."

"You know, it's neat what you said about your dad being like Butch Cassidy."

"I meant it. And I'm going to do a lot more to help

him, too," Roy said. "Now that Angelo is in a wheelchair most of the time, he'll need his kitchen and bathroom remodeled. Dad's going to show me how. Plus there's more volunteer work over at the Wilson farm and Sandy from the YMCA said their basketball hoop is wobbly and needs a new concrete base." Roy was gazing out across the park littered with popcorn and streamers and empty cups. "When you think about it, my dad is more like Butch than I ever was."

"That's not true."

"Yes it is," Roy said, turning back to Jade. He reached out and pushed a pudgy thumb along the edge of the same bumper sticker she was picking at. "So your last day is tomorrow?"

"Yep."

"What are your plans?"

"Aunt Elise was going to take me hiking. Want to come along?"

"I'll bring my parents," Roy said, confident grin blazing. "They'll want to say goodbye, too."

37

Aunt Elise wasn't exaggerating. The meadows along Cottonwood Creek were exploding with brilliant blues and yellows and pinks. Summer flowers crowded between tall strands of golden prairie grass and pushed up against the base of the striking Tetons.

It was like nothing Jade had ever seen. "They're gigantic," she said, referring to the mountains.

"Grand Teton is 13,770 feet above sea level," Aunt Elise said.

Jade looked at the serrated rocky point of Grand Teton extending up into the sky. "I'd like to make that climb someday."

"Count me in," Roy said at her side.

"It will take a good amount of effort and planning," Aunt Elise said. Then she poked the tall walking stick she had brought into the ground and pressed on toward Roy's parents, who were up the path scouting out possible spots for a picnic. Mrs. Parker had brought a basketful of sandwiches and cookies and fruit.

Jade was still looking at the mountain peak.

"How high above sea level is Philly?" Roy asked.

"Something like forty feet. The tallest thing we have is the Comcast building. My class went there on a field trip in fourth grade. It has fifty-seven floors but even then, the building is only nine hundred and seventy-five feet tall."

"Imagine climbing fourteen of those buildings stacked on top of one another," Roy said.

"That would be quite a hike."

"Let's do it! Let's climb Grand Teton! We'll spend the next few summers training and studying the best routes to the top. Elise knows these mountains like she knows her own backyard. How long do you think it will take before we're ready?"

"Aunt Elise said it would take three summers when we were talking about it yesterday," Jade said.

"Then we'll work toward making it to the summit three years from now." Roy reached out. "Deal?"

"Deal," Jade said, shaking his hand.

They continued farther along the trail, which clung to the side of the wide creek and wove in between clusters of pines and out across a broad meadow. After a few minutes, they met up with the Parkers and Aunt Elise, who were busy spreading out a blanket and unpacking the lunch basket.

"You couldn't ask for better weather than this," Mr. Parker said, straightening a corner of the blanket.

"A beautiful send-off for our Jade," Mrs. Parker added. She was laying out an array of sandwiches.

Roy walked over and stood by his dad. "Jade and I just made a pact to climb Grand Teton three summers from now."

The adults stopped their lunch preparations.

"Is that right?" Mr. Parker asked.

"Yep," Roy said. "We figure Elise could be our guide and help us train over the next couple of years."

"I'm game," Aunt Elise said.

"Well." Mrs. Parker went back to pulling shiny red apples from the basket and stacking them on the blanket. "No one is more qualified than Elise when it comes to these mountains and I know teenagers climb that peak all the time. I suppose it will be all right."

"I think it's a brilliant plan," Mr. Parker said. "Something you can look forward to."

Roy and Jade each took a sandwich, apple, and cookie

and then found a rock to sit on over by the creek, away from the others.

"Are you sure you're up for such a big hike?" Roy asked, taking a bite of ham sandwich. "It means you'll have to keep coming back to Wellington."

"I'm trying to be more open to adventure," Jade said. "I used to think it was better hanging out at home and keeping to myself, but then I met this kid who showed me I was wrong. He taught me how important it is to loosen up and have some fun."

"Sounds like a smart kid."

"The smartest." Then she turned her face up and felt the honey light of the sun washing down over her. "I guess Aunt Elise was right," she said, chin pointing heavenward. "Skies like these make you believe you can do anything."

ACKNOWLEDGMENTS

There were times during the work on this novel when I felt as if my supportive agent, Steven Chudney, and my patient editor, Margaret Ferguson, deserved an honorary doctorate in archaeology. Stories can be a challenge to unearth and they helped me find this particular one layer by gentle layer. I would like to thank them and all the wonderful staff at Macmillan. Thanks also go to Lois Moss, Terry Johnson, and Becky Gentry for insight and to Holdman Glass Studios for allowing me to poke around and learn more about the beauty of glass art. I shamelessly stole the names and descriptions for some of the dogs in this novel from my friends and neighbors and am grateful they allowed me to do so. I tried to triple-check my facts on the stories I have heard and loved about the real Butch Cassidy and take sole responsibility for any mistakes I may have made. Finally, I want to thank my loving husband and children for their unfailing support—you are my sunsets, my stars, my rainbow clouds.